Counting The Stars Together

@@#AB0@@

1st Floor, Rajhans Arcade, Mall Road, Kohka, Bhilai, Chhattisgarh 490020

Website: **www.orangebooks.in**

First Edition, 2024

ISBN: 978-93-5621-588-7

Price: Rs. 299

The opinions/ contents expressed in this book are solely of the author and do not represent the opinions/ standings/ thoughts of OrangeBooks.

Printed in India

Counting The Stars Together

PRAKRITI MANDAL

Some things are meant to be...

OrangeBooks Publication
www.orangebooks.in

For my husband, who always pushes me to reach for the stars..

Contents

Chapter 1

Misha

'You know what, I can't cook anything if there is nothing in the fridge!" Ritu Didi shouted on the top of her voice from the kitchen so that my neighbors can know about everything happening here.

Clearly, she is very annoyed today.

Now, it has been 4 days on a row that I forgot to order vegetables. It's not that I was doing it intentionally, it's just that I am supposed to give a very important session tomorrow and my head is way too preoccupied to think of something else.

"Just give me 5 minutes, I will order everything today Ritu didi", I tried to sound childish in front of her. "You can also take leave today evening if you want," I added, just to sugarcoat my last line even more. She smiled and turned towards me saying "Hakka noodles and Veg Manchurian, this would be your dinner, right?"

God! She knows everything! Why she would not though, she is the one who is there, cooking the best home cooked meals for me and taking care of me since last 3 years, the time when I first moved to this place.

No matter how bad or dull my day is, a plate full of Didi's special Biryani can turn everything good. My friends are a fan of her, but that is the major disadvantage for me as all our parties mainly takes place at my 2 BHK! *Although, I avoid parties as much as possible.*

I tried ordering some veggies and fruits while lying on my couch with some extra cushions beneath my feet. This is my habit of lying, I need lots of cushions to rest my feet, which gives me that extra comfort.

I love this small space of mine in this busy hustle bustle of the city, it keeps me calm and happy. My best hobby other than travelling to new places is decorating this small space of mine with happy memories which I collect from everywhere I travel. I chose this life for myself, and I am super proud of that. *Also, I am lonely.*

Loving myself or spending time with myself is still something that I am trying to learn every day. Unleashing the fear of staying alone and covering myself in the threads of a cocoon is what I chose for my life but frankly speaking I am hollow from inside. Whatever I do nowadays, is just to add a layer of sand on my sadness which eventually gets washed off after few days. I want to show myself as a happy girl in the front of the world but cannot escape from those lies in this house. A haunting fear of betrayal still lingers in my mind and often carries me back to my past, which I want to delete from my life.

Indulging in those bitter memories from the past, suddenly made me feel pukish, I wanted to throw up everything but then I try to calm myself down. I stand up, go to the kitchen, and gulp down half a bottle of cold water. Then I come back and switch on my television and start playing my favorite episode from “Friends”.

Monica and Rachel do calm me down, I smiled to myself.

Buzzzz Buzzz.. my phone started vibrating on my coffee table. I lazily pick it up while my eyes glued to the television screen.

Hi Misha, how are you? Radhika’s voice startle me.

I composed myself before answering her. Though despite being my manager, Radhika is really sweet I must say. But still when you have a presentation next day, no sweetness can tackle your fear.

“Hi Radhika, I am good, how is everything?” I tried sounding casual.

“Everything is good, is the presentation ready for tomorrow? Though I don’t have a fraction of doubt on your skills, but just trying to make sure everything is lined up as needed.” She tried to sound as polite as possible, still I can feel a small thread of fear lingering in her voice.

“Yes, the presentation is ready, along with the activities following it up. Also, I am covering Communication and Teamwork topics for tomorrow, and Vikas will be handling Adaptability and Critical thinking for Wednesday." Although she knows everything, but I just reiterated to her to sound more confident.

I am working as a Learning & Development senior specialist in Skills Nurture company located in Hyderabad. Previously I was in the field of HR but slowly I developed an inclination towards giving trainings to people on various issues which we face every day in our corporate lives. *I have developed this story in my mind to forget the actual reason for this change in my career.*

We provide trainings to mainly new joiners in various organizations, speaking of which we have a similar day tomorrow where I am giving training to a group of new joiners in a big, reputed IT firm.

So yes, it's a big day for me indeed. I quickly check the hanging clock, it's 8 PM already! Man, I am watching Friends for last 4 hours!

"I trust you a lot Misha", Radhika's voice brings me back to the ongoing call.

"Also, don't forget about the Q&A section at the end before the commencement of the activities. It's really important this time, as the client is huge for us."

"I won't, don't worry!" I assured her. "Also, I will recheck and go through everything once again tonight to check out if anything is missing at our end".

"Let me also give a quick call to Vikas because as you know he will surely wait for the last moment to finish off with everything!" Radhika laughed.

"Sure, you must do that"! I join with her laughter.

Vikas and I are working together since last 1 year, but we are completely opposite as colleagues. He is more interested in fun and friends and believes to do everything at the last moment and me on the other side is too composed and try to complete everything way before time. But still, we both are great friends, and he is really fun! He cracks the silliest jokes and laughs at himself, which is the funniest part about him!

"Good night, Misha, let's meet tomorrow then!" Radhika continues.

"Good night, Radhika", I smiled and quickly ended the call.

I quickly get up and switch off the television. Grasping the phone in my hand I head towards the washroom to take a quick shower. A much-needed refreshment before I open my laptop and start working again. After a quick 10 minutes shower I change into my comfiest blue-colored night dress, which I have recently purchased from TheGoofy brand, my personal favorite for night suits.

Looking at myself in the mirror I apply my moisturizer and lip balm and smile at myself for looking like a blueberry cake. Adding to the color of the night dress, my eyes are also blue which is giving that extra cherry on the top feeling right now.

Picking up my phone, I quickly swiggyed my favorite Hakka Noodles and Veg Manchurian before starting to work again.

I opened the laptop and sitting cross-legged on my study chair I said to myself "Let's start Misha, you have a big day tomorrow."

Ting tong, ting tong.. I cover my ears with the pillows as the doorbell continues to ring! As the ringing continues, I have no choice but to get up and open the door! It's Meru Didi, one who cleans and does the dishes.

"Meru didi why did you come so early today"? I say as I open the door with my half opened sleepy eyes.

"It's 8.30 Didi, don't you have to go to office today?", She replied with her surprised face.

Oh shit! No No No, it can't be man! How can I be late today? This is just a repercussion of me sleeping at 4.00 AM in the morning! Oh my God, I have to reach office at 9.30 AM, and it includes 30 minutes of traffic which I need to swim across in order to reach my office.

I stay in Kondapur, and my office is in Hitech city, which is around 10 kms away from my place, but in a Monday morning this 10 kms requires around 30 minutes for me to reach office.

Also, I need to quickly call Ritu Didi and tell her not to come today morning, as I am already running late. I will pick up a subway on my way today.

"Late night parties are the reason for your late mornings", Meru Didi passed her unsolicited opinion with a sarcastic smile.

I don't have time for explanations right now, so I ignored her and quickly went inside to get ready. "Oh no, Radhika is going to politely kill me today", I muttered to myself.

I don't know how, but somehow, I managed to reach office at 9.45.

I quickly swiped my card and entered office, where I saw Shweta throwing me a smile from her seat. Shweta and I are besties since last 3 years, and everyone knows about that. We are hardly seen alone, and always together. Be it coffee breaks, or long office gossips, or covering up for each other, we have got each other's back. She is a sweetheart and I adore her. She is my most valued treasure which I earned from this city.

I gestured her saying I will come back in a minute after meeting Radhika. Because right now that's what is triggering in my head.

Me and Radhika are going to Renew Ltd, a big and reputed IT firm in Hyderabad, at 11 AM. We have our scheduled session at 12 PM today.

I spotted Radhika having some discussion with Praveen, she saw me and passed a quick smile. I sighed with relief after seeing that she is not angry with me.

Radhika turned towards me and came forward, "Hi Misha, you are looking pretty today, I must say."

I blushed.

I have worn my favorite purple pencil skirt and white shirt for today's session. I left my hair open, touching my shoulders, and have put minimal and subtle makeup to give that glow. After wearing my black stilettos, I am walking more confidently. So yes, I know that I am looking different today and it got reconfirmed with Radhika's compliment.

"Thank you, Radhika, and same goes for you too", I replied trying to resist that extra beaming smile in my face.

"So, are we ready to kill this time too?" Radhika's encouraging voice made me more confident.

"Let's do it then", I said with a confident smile this time.

"Misha Sharma, it's a big day for you girl", I said to myself.

Chapter 2

Rishi

"Bro trust me it was working fine until last night, I have rerun it twice!" Rohan threw up his hands in the air while twisting his lips, hopelessly trying to sound sad as he says this.

'Let's debug and find what's the issue then!" I sighed. It's been two days now, me and Rohan are working on this stupid code, and we are always stuck in the midway.

"Dude I just hate my job!' I murmured dryly.

"Same bro, same", Rohan sighed.

Rohan and I are more than just work colleagues. We struggle our ass off throughout the week, drink tons of beer in the weekend and make sure to throw the ugliest slangs we know for our Fat & Bad manager and then go back to our shittiest workplace on Monday. Yes, our manger is Fat and Bad, and we mean it! It might sound mean, but he is just so intolerable. He is never happy and trust me, we just see that glint of smile on his face when

Reshmi comes up with some new issue in front of him. He is 42, married with 2 children, but still have his eyes on Reshmi, our team member, without failing. Such a creep!

And, when it comes to me and Rohan, every issue is a silly reason which we are making up in our head, just to avoid work. He is always behind us not giving a single chance to breathe peacefully. So practically we all hate him, including Reshmi. She is also fed up with his oversweet nature towards her which is so annoying sometimes!

Putting his hands around my shoulder Rohan said, "Let's go for a smoke man, my head is so jammed!"

I don't smoke, but I always accompany him just to get a break from this monotony for few minutes.

We went near the lift and pressed the button.

As the lift opened, Kapil, one of our HRs comes out from the lift.

"Oh God! What a timing!", now he is going to for sure say something which I don't want to hear now!" I said to myself.

"Hey Rishi, Hi Rohan, how are you guys? Going for a smoke?" Kapil sounded overexcited!

"Yes we are, do you want to join us"? Rohan replied, and I glared towards him with a look which exactly amplified that "WAS IT VERY NECESSARY TO ASK HIM ROHAN?"

Rohan understood my look and made a "I am sorry" face, which for me was of no use at that point! It was already too late.

"Yes, yes why not!" With a broad smile as usual Kapil was super ready.

As we reached the smoking zone in the basement, Kapil started speaking and I knew he was one who needs no audience and can talk endlessly! I just made a no expression face and stood there, trying to kill the time.

"Today is that training session for the new joiners, you remember, right Rishi?" Kapil turned towards me. I suddenly remembered about the session for which my sweet manager Naveen has as usual asked me to be present and help the team from... wait what was the company's name? I tried to recall...

Before I could recall, Kapil spoke again, "I am talking about the training that SkillsNurture company is giving, you remember right? It's scheduled at 12 PM today."

"Yes I do, but I guess I won't be able to make at 12 PM today, Rohan will occupy my space. Won't you Rohan?" I spoke to him with that look "Say yes, or else no beer night on Saturday!"

"Rishi you know about that call with the Australian client at 12 PM right? I have to be there!" Rohan's words brought back my memory! Oh God! What's happening to me nowadays, why is everything slipping off from my mind?

"Fine, I will be there!" I snapped angrily.

With another 20 minutes of Kapil speaking, we finally came up to our floor. It's already 11.30 now. I quickly went to the coffee machine, took a large cup of cappuccino, and came back to my seat. Taking my laptop and notepad from my seat along with the coffee I started going towards the training rooms.

"Goodluck Bro, Enjoy!" Rohan teased.

I glared at him once before heading towards the training room.

"God, I should have taken 2 mugs of coffee instead of one", I scolded myself, because coffee can only keep me awake in this boring session!

As I approach towards the training room, I can see Naveen with two other girls discussing something. I guess, those two girls are from SkillsNurture. Seeing Naveen smiling so sweetly in front of them just wanted me to punch him on his face! Such a double faced he is!

I can see a face of one of them from outside, who is I am guessing someone senior type, apparently from her glasses and suit attire. And for another one, I can't see her face, her back is turned towards me. But I must say she has really a good choice of dresses! The skirt and shirt are really complimenting her height and figure. "Too much imagination Rishi," I scolded myself.

As I open the door and go inside, the three of them turn towards me.

"Hi, I am Rishi, Senior Developer, for the Devops team", I smiled.

Two girls smiled enthusiastically and came forward to introduce themselves.

Now, that girl wearing purple skirt is standing in front of me. For a moment it was difficult to hold the coffee mug back from spilling over and also to not blink my eyes in front of her.

She is so beautiful man! I mean I am 29, and I have been around lots of girls till now, but she is different. The smile in her face, her cute little nose, and those blue eyes! I mean how can someone have such pretty eyes! Also, her dark brown hair complimenting with her wheatish skin tone is just so beautiful!

I can just keep staring at her throughout the day!

“Hi, I am Misha” her sweet voice slapped me back to the present.

I nervously stretched my hand for a handshake, she could sense my nervousness, I guess. As we shook our hands, I forgot for a second that there are two more people around us.

“Her hands are too soft to be true!” the voice in my head shouted!

“Hi, I am also here!” The other girl’s voice startled me. All three of them had that grin on their faces. I had that sudden urge of running and hiding myself in Mars! Oh God, I am so stupid!

“Sorry, it’s just that..” the fumbling was so clear in my voice.

"No worries I am Radhika, manager from Skills Nurture," she said by cutting my line of embarrassment.

Naveen's white teeth with that yellow tint was more visible today than any time before. Her eyes and teeth both were redirected towards Misha.

"I swear I will kill him someday"! My inner voice snapped.

"So, let's go through everything once again, and connect our laptops with the projector screen as we have just 15 minutes remaining before the new joiners occupy this space" Radhika's voice made everyone active once again.

But not me, I am busy watching Misha through the corner of my eyes, the way she picks up her laptop, the way she sneezes and covers her cute little nose with her palms followed by an "excuse me"!, the way she is readjusting her falling strands of hair on the forehead, everything she does is so cute, so beautiful!

"Do you need any help?" My unannounced voice from behind startled her.

"Everything is done I guess, let's just wait for the new joiners! By the way thanks for asking though, you are really nice" her voice jingled.

"No don't be so sweet, or else I will just grab your face with my hands and plant a kiss on those beautiful lips" stupid voice in my heart started shouting!

"But you are a playboy, remember Rishi? We don't date" the voice in my head always says in the middle! Me and my heart hate him! Ughh..

"Thank you, same goes for you too!", I could only utter these words.

"Who says same goes for you too? You are such an asshole! She will now think that you are a big fool!" My brain scolded me.

She passed a quick smile and then started working in her laptop again.

15 minutes pass by just in a blink of eye and the new joiners starts entering the meeting room. I take one corner seat and as I look at my coffee mug, I smile silently, "I don't need this today, I have a new addiction" my super happy heart shouted!

Chapter 3

Misha

The session went pretty well.

The new joiners seemed to have enjoyed the session and there were less yawns comparatively! We had an interactive Q&A session at the end followed by some small interactive games with them. Naveen, the manager of the team appears to be happy with us, I must say extra happy than usual! He is smiling unnecessarily which is irritating sometimes. Nevertheless, I am not coming back in this office anytime soon so nothing to worry about much.

Radhika seems to be super happy though!

"I guess we have got a permanent client now, all the upcoming sessions of this company are coming to us only! All credit goes to you Misha, you were incredible today!" Radhika spoke without a single pause.

My heart swelled.

"Thank you for trusting me Radhika! I love this job.." Before I could finish my sentence, someone's "excuse me" from behind interrupted me. I turned back.

"You did such a fantastic job today, the session was really good! It was not at all boring as before, good job Misha!" the extra sweet tone of Rishi standing in front of me startled me a bit.

"Is he trying to flirt with you, Misha"? mini-Misha is now activated in my head. This mini-me version keeps chattering about every person or every situation I am currently in.

"I don't know, and I am not interested too!", I scolded mini-me. "*But he is sooo handsome, also his smile is so sexy, Misha, he is a stud dude, just go and speak with him*!"

"Stop, just stop, you know I want to be single throughout my life, right? Just remember your past and stop expecting anything", I spoke harshly with myself because it starts forgetting the past.

But somehow mini-me was right this time. Indeed, Rishi was trying to flirt with me which I can understand since last 3 hours. His eyes were glued towards me throughout the session. A girl's sixth sense, you know? No matter wherever we are looking, we can sense easily if someone is staring at us! But in spite of him being handsome and attractive, I have no intention to entertain him. I keep myself miles away from dating and stuff ever since that incident took place 3 years back, where the person whom I trusted with everything had broken my faith, my heart, my all. I have lost faith in love. Friendships are fine, but not anything more than that is approved by my head or heart.

It's empty and hollow.

"Did I say something wrong?" Rishi's voice dragged me back to the conversation! *"Misha that poor boy doesn't know about any shit in your life, so please behave!"*, Mini-me reminded me.

"No no, I am so sorry, my mind was somewhere else. Thanks for your compliment though, means a lot." I tried sounding sweet.

"So, how long have you been working with SkillsNurture?" Rishi is trying to have a conversation now! *"Don't be weird, don't be weird, please, just answer to his questions and head back from here!"*, Mini-me begs.

"Two years!" I replied.

Ohh.. I have been working in Renew for 3 years now, before that.." cutting his words in the middle I fumbled "Actually I need to go to my manager, she was asking for some details, sorry for interrupting you, bye!".

Without giving him a chance to speak again, I turn backwards and start walking towards Radhika. I am practically running, I must say.

"Should we go for lunch?" I asked Radhika.

I need an escape plan.

"Yes sure, let's go! I have heard that this office campus nests some amazing cafes, we can go and have something there, shall we?" Radhika asked.

"Yes yes, sure, anything will do" I smiled.

This office campus is pretty good I must admit. It has lush green lawns around, vibrant colored pavements and pretty cafes, surrounded by sky kissing corporate buildings with those beautiful glass exteriors. Our campus is relatively smaller than this. But this place runs my memory back to 3 years, where my previous organization had somewhat similar campus like this. I have numerous memories attached with that place. And every memory has Kunal etched in it.

Kunal, this name brings back thousands of memories, some are too good to be forgotten and most are too bad to be remembered.

Kunal and I met each other in my previous organization. I was in the HR team, and he was in the Marketing team. We interacted few times casually, until we properly met in an office party one day. We were all not sober, too drunk to get a hold of anything happening around us. I remembered dancing crazily with the music along with my friends. Suddenly, I saw Kunal coming towards me. Those brown eyes were telling me a lot of things.

"You are so pretty", was his first few words.

"Will you dance with me?", were the next ones.

My mind was not working properly, and I was way too much happy that day. I started dancing with him, and I was having so much fun!

His hands were holding my waist and my hands covering his shoulders. We were swaying through the tunes of the music, and I still clearly remember "A thousand years" by Christina Perri being played in the background. Bringing his lips close to my ears Kunal asked, "Will you have dinner with me tomorrow?" I blushed and nodded. This marked the start of our 6 months romantic period, where we shared countless of happy memories, until the day I came to know about the truth.

"Please please don't go back there, I don't want to remember all those things!" I pleaded to my brain. "Just press Ctrl+Alt+Dlt, pleaseeeee!"

"Will you please stop moving to the past, and enjoy the lunch you are going to have now?" Mini-me is not always bad though!

"Should we go to The Enchanted Soul Café?, It looks pretty!" Radhika asked turning towards me.

"Yes, it's beautiful, let's go there"! Even though my mind is screwed up now, but I need to be happy!

"Misha you need to enjoy your present moment!" I keep reminding myself!

We ordered some pink sauce pasta, roasted vegetables and two mocktails. Virgin Margarita for me as it's my favorite, and Blueberry Mojito for Radhika.

"Can we also join?", a familiar voice startled us. It's Rishi and an unknown boy, who looked similar to Harry Potter!

"*Is he following you? If yes, then he is such a sweetheart Misha, please don't mess this up now!"* Mini-me started dancing salsa right now! I hate her!

"Yes sure, please join us!" Radhika is over-polite now.

I am super angry.

"Hi, I am Rohan", the other guy, doppelganger of Harry Potter, introduced him. "Me, and Rishi work in the same team and we are good friends", he continued.

Now this information was not much needed though. *"Behave Misha!"* mini-me reminded again.

So, have you guys already ordered something? Rishi asked looking at me.

"Umm..yes, pasta and roasted vegetables and some mocktails". I hesitatingly replied.

"Great! I love pasta too!", Rishi added. Rohan pushed him with his elbow and spoke in a low voice "Bro, you hate pasta, don't act over smart, let's order Biryani, I am starving."

I pressed my lips to hold back my smile.

"Excuse me, your order Sir?", the waiter started asking Rishi & Rohan. Before Rohan could say anything Rishi said, "Just double the order both of them placed", by pointing his finger towards us.

Rohan glared towards Rishi, and I controlled my laugh somehow.

"Idiot!" my mind smiled.

"So, this café looks pretty cool though!" Radhika searched for topics.

"Yes it is, there are few more interesting cafes here. Next time whenever you guys come, we can take you there!" Rishi smiled.

"*Is he indirectly asking you to go out with him? I mean you can go for a small coffee date, it's no harm really!"* Mini-me is overexcited!

I just want to run away from here now.

Thank God, the food arrived early, and we all started eating silently. Although, I can sense those pair of eyes secretly scanning me. I can see both of them struggling to finish off the pasta, and their expressions clearly proves that they hate pasta! Haha! These boys are so silly man, can literally do anything to impress us!

Finishing off our food, we split the bills amongst ourselves and start moving towards the exit door.

"Is there any washroom nearby"? Radhika asked both of them.

Rishi springed up and said, "Rohan can you please show Radhika the way to the washroom?"

Rohan threw an angry look towards Rishi and said "Yes, sure."

"Oh God! Please make me invisible, please please!", I started panicking.

"So, I can see you are trying to avoid me, is there any particular reason behind it?" Rishi is now becoming annoying!

"Nothing as such, we hardly know each other and how can you expect me to hang around with you and give you all my attention?" I sounded rude, but it's okay. He deserves it.

"But girls whom I frequently meet, die to talk with me after our first interaction only! Because I am so handsome, you know?" He grinned, and I swear, I just wanted to stab him.

I look at him sternly and say, "I am not one of them and I have a lot of work to do, can you please leave me alone?", the irritation in my voice was quite obvious now.

"You are rude! I like rude girls!" This boy is just too much now.

"And you are a self-obsessed prick" I twist my lips.

"Ouch, that was quite hurtful" he replies.

"Boy, if you don't want to get hurt anymore then please stay away from me" my brain shouted at him.

I see Radhika and Rohan approaching us. I breathed a sigh of relief.

Before Radhika could say something, I said "Let's go Radhika, we are running late! I have some pending work to finish off today".

Radhika looked at me and she could read my unspoken thoughts, "Yes, yes let's go", she replied.

"So, when will be the next session?", Rishi asked Radhika. I very well know what his intention is!

"On Wednesday, day after tomorrow. Another colleague of ours, Vikas will be giving the training, and I will come with him." Hearing Radhika's words changed Rishi's excitement to sadness.

"Ohh.. okay, will meet Wednesday then! Bye!"

"Since when you have started to be so enthusiastic about sessions bro?" I overheard Rohan asking Rishi.

"Since today, do you have any problem?", Rishi hissed back.

I waved a fake smile back towards them, and me and Radhika started walking towards the parking zone. Radhika owns a Seltos, and she drives daily to the office. The car is black in color, and I really love it.

"Someday I will also own one!" I say to myself after stepping inside the car.

A lot of things are going on in my head right now and I need to vomit everything once I meet Shweta in the office today. She is the one who listens to me patiently without passing any judgements. We hold a huge place in each other's hearts. She is my best friend, I love her. Glad to have found someone to share everything with, whenever I need. I don't know what I would have done without her.

Just somehow this day needs to end, it's a super anxious day for me!

As we reached office, I ran towards Shweta. Thankfully she was free that time, surfing something on her phone. I started panting as I reached her.

"What happened, are you alright? How was your session, things didn't land up well?" bombardment of questions were thrown towards me.

"I am good, session was pretty good. But there is something else which I need to discuss", I panicked. "Carry on", Shweta said. I narrated the whole incident which happened in ReNew, focusing on some specific details about Rishi and how I feel that it's just the beginning of the story, there is just so much more upcoming to it.

Shweta listened attentively to everything, and after passing her water bottle towards me opened her mouth to speak.

“It’s okay to feel like this sometimes, but don’t overthink or overstress yourself. See, I understand you have a very bad experience in the past which is haunting you always no matter what. But that doesn't mean you are going to overanalyze every small move in your life. Secondly, all guys are not Kunal”.

I narrowed my eyes, as I don’t want her to behave like my mini-me for now.

“Just, I mean to say, enjoy the attention you are getting. Flirting is healthy babe, no one is getting harmed in it. Nobody is asking you to marry Rishi, right? Just go with the flow, and don’t think too much about it. And adding to everything, you always have my back sweetie, so chill! Will you have beer tonight?” Shweta’s long speech somewhat calmed my nerves.

“Beer & Netflix, then?” I smiled.

“Yaaaay! done”, Shweta & I have a plan now!

As I go back to my seat, I feel much better than before. Finishing few pending works, I close my laptop and start getting ready to leave for the day. Before leaving, I remind Shweta about today’s plan, and she said she will reach by 9 at my place.

As I sit in my cab, my phone starts ringing. I check, it’s Mom’s call. I quickly pick it up.

“How are you beta?”, this baby tone of her is always to make me smile.

"I am good mom, how is everything at home?, did dad come back home from college?", I ask her.

So, I am born and brought up in Delhi. My dad is a professor and mom is a teacher. I am their single child, and they have brought me up with lots of freedom and never for once made me feel that I am any lesser than a boy. They have let me choose which ever field I wanted and encouraged me to get out from my comfort zone and chase my dreams. Also, they never forced me for anything, just acted as wind beneath my wings which helped me to fly more.

I spoke with her for few minutes and then ended the call. I am about to reach home in next 20 minutes I guess.

Will need to take a long hot bath and will ask Meru didi to make my favorite Aloo Parathas today for dinner. Shweta loves them too! I thought to myself.

Ultimately it's going to be a happy night I guess!

Chapter 4

Rishi

It's been two days since I met her.

Two long days of thinking about her in every second, two long days of constantly trying to concentrate on other things, but in vain.

She has occupied my whole mind, and I don't know how.

It's not that I have not met prettier girls before, or I have not dated someone earlier, but she is different. Those eyes speaks thousands of words which I want to read. That smile carry some unresolved pain which I want to wash away. But how can she create such magic in just 2 hours?

It feels like I have been hallucinated.

"Bro, please don't litter the living space with those crumbled packets of chips! I can't just run behind you and keep cleaning the house!" Varun's lecture started again.

Varun and I are staying in this 2BHK since last 2 years now. We both are really good friends, just subtracting the fact that he wants everything to be freaking clean always and, me on the other hand can just procrastinate in my bed throughout the day, no matter how unclean the room is. Keeping this thing aside, we both are brothers for lifetime. We are both die hard Barcelona fans, and we love to travel to new places whenever we gather some time.

Me and Varun met through a common flat hunting group on Facebook, where Varun was looking for a flatmate and I was searching for a good place to stay. Previously, before 2 years I used to stay in a shitty boy's hostel and somehow after staying there for a year I was desperately looking for a good place to move in.

Luckily I got this flat, and Varun as my flatmate.

He is from Ludhiana, and I am from Chandigarh. Both being Punjabi, we click together beautifully.

Ignoring Varun's speech on how we should keep our living room clean, I continued to scroll my phone. I am checking the Instagram profile of Misha since the last two days now, all thanks to the Almighty that it's a public profile, not a private one.

I stare at every picture of her profile for 5 minutes each.

It has become a ritual now, since last 2 days.

I am just contemplating whether or not I should hit my finger on the message icon and send a "Hi" to her. "Will it seem to be very desperate?", my voice in head was very doubtful.

"Just send it bro, don't think too much!" Varun's voice just shook me up.

"Bro , you are peeping into my phone? I will kill you!" I shouted back.

"Bro, you are just in a different zone for 2 days now, and I can understand she is not any usual type. I have never seen you like this before. So just send a "Hi" and don't overthink it now! Keep doing hard work and don't worry about the result!" He threw the last sentence with his hands up in the air, just like a renowned preacher.

I smiled and punched him lightly with my fist. But in the back of my mind, I desperately wanted to send a message. Something brave snapped inside me, and I just typed "Hi"!

OH GOD!, now there is no turning back from here. Why did I do this?

I can see that the message got delivered but she is not active right now. Now my screentime will just increase 10 times more, as I will keep staring at the phone until she replies. *If she replies at all.*

It's 7 PM, Wednesday evening, I came back home at 5.30 PM today, so I can work the remaining bit from home. *Which I actually didn't!*

Varun is doing work from home nowadays, so I sometimes come back early from office, just to give him company.

"Bro let's go and have Chicken Kurkure Momo's, I am super hungry", Varun's words sounded as the perfect escape plan from my super anxious mind which is asking me to recheck my phone every 2 seconds.

I jumped up and agreed.

Varun has a scooty, which we both use to roam about in Hyderabad, especially late nights. Right now, we are going to the food street opposite to DLF cyber city. Staying in Gachibowli gives us this advantage of having our office and some pretty good street food options, both in our proximity.

DLF cyber city is just 5 mins ride from our society.

As, we reach the place, I checked my phone once again before heading towards the Momo's junction. Suddenly the 'seen' word below my message forced my legs to stop from moving farther.

She didn't reply.

Without losing hope suddenly my mind thought of something very funny.

Why not send her some silly updates from my day, maybe she would block me after that or maybe she would find me funny and reply back. Who knows?

Crossing my fingers, I started off with my mission.

Mission: To irritate her so much that she is bound to give a reply, even if it's an angry one!

I started typing, "Hi Misha, I know you don't want to talk with a self-obsessed prick like me, but I want to talk with you a lot, so how about sharing with you some live updates from my life? I know somewhere or the other you are intrigued too, right?" I press the send button.

In few seconds I can see, seen below my message. I smiled to myself.

The game is ON.

I see Varun, with an angry face coming towards me. Oh shit! He has asked me to order the Momo's till the time he parks his scooty. But as usual, I was busy!

"You didn't order Momo's right? Don't know what magic that girl has spelled on you dude!" He snapped! "And stop smiling like a fucking idiot now, and let's order the Momo's, I am starving!" He continued.

"Let's go bro, it's just that I didn't want the Momo's to get cold before you come back, you know?", my lie was pretty obvious, and Varun's glare reconfirmed it.

We ordered one plate of chicken Kurkure Momo's and one plate of Paneer Tandoori Momo's, both being our favorite. Also, we picked up a small bottle of coke from a nearby shop and started waiting for our order to arrive.

Meanwhile, Varun's phone started ringing. "Who is it?", I asked.

He checked and replied, "Sushant from college", and then he picked up and started talking.

I quickly started typing again, as I have few minutes before the order arrives.

I started typing, "So Misha, I am currently standing in front of Momo's delight, opposite to DLF cybercity. The Momo's here are just so awesome! Have you ever tried them?"

I hit an enter, and can see again after few seconds, 'seen' below my message.

"*If she hated you, she would have blocked you after the very first message, right*?", voice in my head was logically happy now!

So, it's working.

By then, our Momo's arrived, and Varun has also ended his call. We both threw ourselves on the plates and without wasting any seconds in between we finished all of them in just 5 minutes! We both ate them as if like we have not eaten since ages! Once finished, Varun asks, "So, that's all right? We need to finish the dinner also which Veena didi made at home."

Yes he is right, Veena Didi is our cook, and although she is really nice and cooks amazing food, but she hates wasting food. Days she sees food is getting wasted and needs to be thrown away, she starts scolding us and throwing some repetitive lines of her, which we have already heard thousands of times.

Remembering those lines, I got scared and answered Varun "No, no nothing more. Let's go home, will have dinner straightaway".

So, we both started heading back towards our home.

I quickly typed another message to Misha, while sitting behind Varun on Scooty.

"Do you like late night scooty rides? I just love them! Currently me and my flatmate are coming back home, and we are enjoying a fun scooty ride!" I send it.

I waited for few seconds, but I see it got delivered but not seen. *Maybe she is having dinner, right?*

Reaching back home Varun announced while taking off his shoes, "Bro, I have an office con call after 10 minutes, got a message from my manager few minutes ago. I guess, there are some immediate changes to be made on the script, our team is working on. The call will get over in an hour, so we can have dinner at around 10 PM, cool?"

"Oh, sure, no worries. Will watch few episodes on Netflix till then, just let me know once your call gets over, okay?" I spoke.

"Yes definitely! Also, other than Netflix, you can message her too", he winked while saying this and started walking towards his room.

"Asshole!" I murmured to myself and went back to my room.

But I guess Varun was right, messaging her is a better option than Netflix, right?

Chapter 5

Misha

"Do you want me to reheat the biryani? It's already 10 PM, and I am now super hungry", Shweta's voice was quite grumpy, I must say.

I can fathom her hunger now!

"Okay, let's just finish this episode, 7 minutes to go. We can have dinner post that", I replied.

"Fine!", Shweta made a sad face and turned towards the television.

We are watching this Sci-fi series in Netflix, and I must say I don't remember anything that happened in the last few episodes. My eyes are continuously switching between my phone and the TV, because of this stubborn guy, so called Rishi. He has already created a lot of nuisances in my head in the last few days, with the thoughts my mind have painted imagining him. I tried a lot to kick him out from my system like I have previously done for a lot of men, but this time it's becoming difficult. Now as a cherry on the top, out of nowhere he has started to message me on Instagram since today evening. In spite of me not giving a single reply, he is providing me with some unnecessary updates of his day which I don't know why. *But still, I am looking at my phone after every 5 minutes, to check if a new update is there!*

I am such a big dumbass! "*But Misha, I am having a feeling that you have already started developing a soft corner in your heart for him, don't you?*" This little me will never understand when to say what!

Although, she is annoyingly right most of the time. *Including this one!*

I am lying on the sofa and have covered myself with my favorite quilt, which is keeping me warm in this chilly 16 degrees AC temperature, also it's helping me to hide my phone from Shweta as I am peeping into it to check the messages.

Shweta comes to my place at least 4 times a week. She stays with her mom, just 2 blocks away from my flat. The major reason for me to shift to this place was because I wanted to stay close to her. We both met 3 years back in my first organization, and luckily we became friends in just few days and there was no turning back since then. Even we switched to the same organization 2 years ago, me at first followed by her after 2 months.

She is the sweetest best friend, everyone wishes to have! And I am that Lucky one.

Also, she witnessed me going through the worst phase of my life two years ago and pulling me out of that traumatic phase was not easy at all.

She has seen me before and after Kunal happened in my life, and she knows how much it affected me. My heart has this big hole now, which throws out everything coming into it. My eyes have lost that glitter and lips have lost its genuine curves.

Trusting someone is not even an option left in my life anymore.

As my best friend, it's difficult for her to see me like this, which I get very easily. She wants me to go for dates, to enjoy life by dragging myself out from my shell, to be that lively Misha which is even difficult for me to remember sometimes.

So, the moment I told her about Rishi few days back, I saw that hope in her eyes again. She wanted me to taste that joy, which is obviously not in my to do list, and I don't know whether it will be back again or not.

To show my vulnerability, is perhaps my biggest fear.

Because of this, I have not shared anything with her about Rishi after that, as I don't want her hopes to rise at all. So, for now, I am just hiding my goofing smile by reading these stupid updates from this silly boy.

As the series gets wrapped up, Shweta springs up from the couch and runs towards the kitchen. I also join her. We both start having dinner, and 5 minutes down my phone starts vibrating with new incoming messages. I quickly pick up my phone to switch off the internet.

"Bro, your phone is vibrating a lot today, isn't it?", Shweta's sarcastic voice has so many questions attached to it.

"It's just work, I have this new session coming up, so Radhika is just sharing some requisites with me for preparation." I lied.

"Oh, Okay, cool" Shweta replied promptly before concentrating back to her Chicken Biryani. "Kudos Misha, sometimes you do lie pretty well!" I high fived myself.

Post dinner, Shweta started preparing to leave. "Are you leaving? Won't you stay today?"

Shweta has her spare clothes in my apartment and most of the times she stays back at my place only. Aunty knows about us very well, so she never has an issue with it.

"I have to go today, as I have this new project to work on from tomorrow, and for that I need to study a bit. You remember about that new project I was talking about right?" Shweta said.

"Yes, yes, I remember. Fine, you leave then and text me once you reach. We will meet tomorrow, in office." I tightly hugged her by saying this.

"I am just going 2 blocks away, chill!", she tried to lighten my mood.

Once she left, I locked the door and went to the bedroom. Lying down, I checked my phone, there were 4 unread messages from Rishi.

Shweta's not staying back today was somewhat manifested by me only, I guess! "*Now we are talking!*" Mini me jumped up!

"So, as I was saying, it has started raining here now!"

"Me and my flatmate Varun, we finished our dinner few minutes back."

"We had Rajma Chawal for dinner today, which is Varun's favorite. But I prefer Chhole Rice more, what about you?"

"By the way, did I mention already that purple color just looks amazing on you?"

Rishi's messages flooded my screen, and I can't help but smile. "*Just talking with him doesn't mean you are dating him, right? He can also be a good friend, just wave off your fatalistic thoughts for once Misha!* Mini-me was charged up.

Fidgeting with my phone for next couple of minutes, I finally decided to reply. "*Blocking him is always an open option, so no need to worry*!" I reassured my anxious soul.

I picked up my phone and started typing..

Me: I never thought that software techies can be so bored with their job, that they need to randomly share their life updates with someone just to kill their time! I hit the send button.

A sudden uncanny fear ran through my spine.

In just few seconds my phone blinked again, with a new message.

Rishi: Someone for the first time comprehended my pain! I am so bored in life that I went outside and pressed the calling bell on my own front door, then I ran back in and asked, "Who is it?"

This silly joke had me in splits! He is stupid. *And also, funny.*

Me: Try cracking something funnier next time, this didn't work.

Rishi: But you are still laughing! So, I guess it worked pretty well.

"*He is pretty good with flirting, I must admit*!" Mini me whispered.

Me: Can I ask something?

Rishi: I'm all ears, always :)

Me: Why are you so eager to talk with me? I guess you should waste your precious time behind girls who are waiting for you, and you can easily strike me off from that list.

Rishi: Hahaha! You are funny too! Not as boring as I thought of! If I say that I visualized a wonderful friend behind that grumpy face of yours, and want to genuinely be friends with her, will you believe me?

I gasped a quick breath of relief. "*Friendship is harmless Misha, just go for it*!" Mini me can never be at peace.

Me: Just a quick rectification: I am not grumpy!

Rishi: Haha! You need to prove it then!

Me: Should I now just make a video with the heading: Top 5 reasons to prove Misha is not grumpy?

Rishi: Nice idea, but it will consume lot of efforts. So why not, just have a coffee with me tomorrow evening and explain the points face to face? ;)

Now he is moving too fast. No, No Misha, we can't meet him, you know how broken you are, and you are beyond repair! My body starts panicking.

I don't reply.

After few seconds my phone beeped.

I don't check.

It beeps again.

Fuck it! Just check your phone Misha! You are overthinking beyond limits now! I gulp half a bottle of water and check my phone.

4 unread messages.

Rishi: Did I cross any line? It's completely fine if you don't want to meet.

Rishi: I just wanted to be friends with you, bothering you was never a call.

Rishi: I am really sorry, we won't meet until you are comfortable, or you decide to meet.

Rishi: Can you please reply? Now you are scaring the life out of me :(

Me: Roast Café, at 5 PM tomorrow, works for you?

Rishi: Man, you just petrified me! Obviously it works for me, I start my countdown from this hour! Thank you for saying Yes!

Me: I wanted to prove that I am not Grumpy, you know?

Rishi: Somewhat convinced, rest I will once we meet.

Me: I guess I will buzz off now, it's already 12 AM, I have an early morning tomorrow. Good night :)

Rishi: Good night, I will wait for tomorrow!

Rishi: By the way, are we going to talk via Instagram only or will I be getting your mobile number too?

I smiled.

Me: Not so soon, will see.

Rishi: Grumpy Misha is back again! Fine, will wait for it. Until then, Bye, Goodnight :)

Me: Goodnight.

I kept my phone on the side table and readjusted myself between the pillows. I love to have lots of pillows on my bed, it kind of helps me to deal with my loneliness. Also, I have recently started going to my office gym occasionally, mainly during the evening hours and my legs are always pretty sure to remind me how weak they are throughout the nighttime.

Thousands of thoughts are running at a high speed in my mind right now, and I know, I won't be able to sleep today. Rishi is the first guy in last 2 years with whom I have agreed to meet. I don't know what pushed me to say yes today, maybe his way to deal with my grumpiness and making small efforts to bring that smile on my face, maybe his way of flirting, which is hilarious, maybe my lonely life, which was searching for someone to talk with, maybe, no sorry, it's actually the most important point that he is really cute! *Apologies it was not me but mini-me speaking the last line!*

But still that haunting incident from the past is killing my nerves. Can the pain ever get better?

Next morning flew in a jiffy. As usual I woke up late at 8.30 AM by the voice of Meru Didi shouting behind the door, along with pressing the calling bell thousands of times.

Ritu didi also came after 10 minutes.

"Just make plain butter toast and coffee for breakfast, and roti with any vegetable you want for lunch" I blabbered in hurry.

"Will make only fried potatoes with roti for lunch, as there is no vegetable in fridge!" Ritu Didi shouted.

Oh shit! I have completely forgotten to order vegetables again! Adulting is pretty hard, really!

I quickly took a shower and opened my wardrobe to decide my clothes. Now it's a tough choice today! I need to wear something simple yet pretty so that it doesn't seem to Rishi that I am too eager to meet him! I reminded myself.

I picked up a blue colored top and paired it up with white trousers. I tied my hair in tight ponytail and wore my favorite nude heels along with. Small pair of rose gold hoops glammed up the entire attire. Using some minimal makeup and putting on my favorite nude pink lip color, completed the entire look.

"Not bad Misha", I said to myself.

After 2 long years, finally, I am trying to peep out from my burrow, which is obviously not going to be easy.

So definitely I will be having a raging heartbeat throughout the day.

Chapter 6

Rishi

I am dancing on cloud 9 today!

I really didn't expect her to reply yesterday, but it did happen. I couldn't sleep the entire night, eagerly waiting for the clock to tick 9 and then to throw myself out of the flat to start the day.

The broad smile on my face is a serious issue for the day! Varun & Rohan will be a real pain in the ass today.

I wore my favorite white t-shirt with a pair of blue denims and white sneakers and looked at myself in the mirror! Not bad Rishi, you can impress any girl in the blink of an eye!

But I remembered myself, that Misha is just not like every other girl. She is different. Her eyes holds lots of stories and it's somewhat difficult for her to trust anyone. Becoming friends with her is not going to be easy, she needs to be handled with lots of care and patience. But one thing I am sure about, that at any cost, I will not give her a chance to regret about the decision she made for meeting with me today.

Her eyes only deserves to shine, nothing more and nothing less.

As I reached office at 10.30, I could see Rohan & Naveen discussing on something which seems to be serious. Well, Naveen never smiles in front of us, so I guess it's not something to worry about. As I approach towards them, I can hear Rohan saying "Naveen, just give me 2 hours, I will work with the team once and will fix this!"

"The client is just sitting on my head, do it ASAP, I don't want any delay on this!" Naveen's voice is sometimes so intolerable!

Saying this he started walking towards his cabin, Thank God! he didn't see me standing behind him.

"What happened now?", I asked Rohan.

"The project we were supposed to deliver today, has some new blockers in it! The testing team took 2 whole days and came up last moment detecting this new fault in the code! Now we were supposed to present it to the client at 11 AM today, but I guess it will take 2-3 hours to fix this issue!", Rohan turned his laptop towards me to show the issue.

There is this webpage in the project which has a field that will auto populate the User's type of credit/debit card according to the last 4 digits of his/her card. It is working for all of the card types, but failing in case of a Mastercard, it's showing "Invalid card number".

I hate my job sometimes! These technical glitches are sometimes just too overwhelming to handle. Going through the code once again and to find that small error is a real pain in the ass. Anyways, there is no way of running back now, so me and Rohan sit together to debug the code once again and find that fucking error.

Misha is constantly running in the back of my mind, it will be really difficult to concentrate here now!

After 1.5 hours of struggle, ultimately we debugged the issue and fixed it. We ran it twice in our system to reconfirm that it's working smoothly. Now we are ready for presenting it to the client at 1 PM.

4 hours to go for meeting Misha. I smiled.

The longest 4 hours of my life.

The presentation went smoothly though, and the client seemed happy. As usual, Naveen didn't say anything good to us, apart from the fact that he reminded us 100 times that, it was our fault due to which this client meeting was postponed for 2 hours!

"Such a looser he is!", Rohan and I said this through our exchanged looks!

"Let's go for lunch dude, I didn't have my breakfast today and I am starving!", Rohan announced!

"Let's go, I guess I have brought your favorite pumpkin for lunch today!", I grinned.

Rohan hates pumpkin perhaps the most in this world! He made an awkward face and said, “I am ordering pizza then!”

“Chill, I have brought Veg Pulao and Dum Aloo today, lets dive into it!” Rohan has shifted to a new place and don’t have a cook as of now. So, I bring extra lunch, so that we both can share, also Rohan loves Veena didi’s delicacies.

“Yaaaay, let’s go then bro!”, Rohan’s 100-watt smile made me happy too. We both started moving towards our cafeteria which is on the 11th floor of the building.

“It’s 2 PM, 3 more hours to go!”, my brain whispered to my ears.

I tried to control my excitement as much as possible.

After a long wait of almost 2.5 hours, the clock ticked 4.20 PM. Now at this very second, if someone gauges the radius of my smile, it would apparently be out of the scale. I quickly dropped a message to Naveen mentioning that I will leave office early today, due to some personal work. Got a reply from him “Okay”.

He knows how much we work our ass off every day, so he is left with no better option other than agreeing to me, though I can understand that he is clearly pissed off by my message. But who cares!

Roast café is just a drive of 10 mins from my office, so I can reach by 4.45 PM easily.

I lied to Rohan also, before leaving, and told him that Varun is asking me to come back home due to some work. I don’t want to disclose anything about Misha to anyone as of now, as I am not sure how things will turn out after today.

Let's for now cross the fingers and hope for the best!

I thought about a lot yesterday that what should I gift her on our first meeting. But nothing apparently crossed my mind which I felt she would like. I didn't want to overstep on anything. After thinking about it for long, finally I went to my book's cabinet and took out my favorite box – "My collection of magnets". This is something which I am doing since my childhood days. I love travelling to new places, and the first thing I search for, whenever I visit a place is a Magnet. It helps me to keep those memories close to my heart. I have covered lots of places in India, which mainly includes hill stations as I love trekking, it's my passion, it drives my life like a fuel.

I have never shared a single magnet with anyone, but I don't know why I wanted to share this time. I picked up a very beautiful magnet from my Manali trip's collection, which is really close to my heart. The magnet holds a picture from the place called Solang valley, in Manali, where I witnessed the first snow fall in my life. So, this magnet brings back all those memories of the first ever snowflakes falling on my nose. Don't know why, but I wanted to share this with Misha.

Will she find me stupid? Will find out today, I guess!

Keeping the magnet back in my pocket, I parked my car in the road, opposite to the café. It's 4.50 PM now, unpredictable traffic took those extra 5 minutes!

As I came out of my car, suddenly my eyes fell on this little girl, wearing this cute pink dress and trying to cross the road. She is probably around 5-6 years old. I quickly turned my eyes to the other side of the road where I can see another girl, slightly older than her, maybe around 11-12 years old who is gesturing to this little girl to wait until she comes to this side and help her in crossing the road. She is probably her elder sister. I quickly took her in my arms and helped her to cross the road and reunite with her sister. Her sister started thanking me and said that, by mistake she crossed the road first without holding her sister's hand which eventually left her behind!

The little girl with her pouty lips says cutely "I can cross the road on my own, I don't need anyone's help! I am a big girl now, you know?"

Controlling my laughter, I said "You are a big girl I know, but still, you need to be big as your sister at least, before you can cross roads on your own, okay? Till then, never leave your sister's hand."

She nodded, but from her expression, I can clearly say she is not convinced. Both of them waved back to me before I started going towards the café.

Just before entering the café, I can see Misha is standing, looking at me. I froze for few seconds. She is looking so pretty, and different today. My eyes and lips are beaming with smile as I reach her. Before I could say anything, she says, "Those two girls were so beautiful! You really did a nice job by helping them!", she smiled.

She is standing here since last 5 minutes!, that's interesting!

"The poor little girl was struggling a lot to cross the road, but apparently according to her she is a big girl and doesn't need anyone's help!", I laughed.

She joined my laughter. *I could see her laughing throughout the day!*

We both went inside and took a table towards the corner. This café has this beautiful greenery inside it, and some pretty lights hanging from above. I visited this café once before, in one of our office parties and I must say that I instantly loved the ambience. But today with Misha sitting in front of me, this place have turned out to be my favorite café in the world!

"Stop staring at her and start a conversation idiot!", my heart started teasing me.

My brain started juggling with topics, unable to decide one! Misha on the other hand is checking her phone and typing something. As I was about to open my mouth to speak, the waiter approached us to take our order.

"I heard that Classic Mac & Cheese Bake Pasta is quite a hype here", I tried to sound like one of those fancy food bloggers having high expertise in food!

"I clearly found your love for pasta in our last meet, so stop pretending anymore, we can have something else!", she smiled.

I blushed!

After going through the menu few times more, we finally ordered one Peri Peri Chicken Pizza and two Iced Cappuccinos, and one Nutella Waffle on Misha's request. Misha has a sweet tooth, I can confidently vouch on that!

"So, are you a frequent comer in this café?" I tried to initiate a conversation.

"This café is just 10 minutes away from my office, so me and my friend Shweta often come here to have the Classic Mac & Cheese Bake Pasta, which is really good!", saying this she winked!

She just reconfirmed that I am indeed a big Idiot!

"Now it seems that you are not as grumpy as I thought of!", I tried to change the conversation to avoid my embarrassment!

"Sometimes you need to put on a mask, right?", she sighed.

"But for someone who holds such a beautiful smile, grumpiness can never be an option!"

"How can someone be so cheesy!", she narrowed her eyes.

"But still, you are liking it, I can see!"

Hearing my words, a subtle laugh leaves through Misha's chest. "You are really so self-obsessed man!"

"Loving yourself can always be a happy obsession!", I sounded like some motivational speaker!

"Not everyone can practice this obsession, I guess!", her eyes again threw thousands of unanswered questions which I saw on the first day I met her.

Her eyes hold some kind of unresolved pain, which is always searching for answers.

"Excuse me Sir, Excuse me Ma'am, here's your food", waiter's voice broke that stare between us.

As the waiter served our food, we started eating it and once again an awkward silence covered up our space.

"So, you and Shweta are flat mates?", I tried diverting the topic.

"No, I stay alone, and Shweta stays with her Mom 2 blocks away from my place".

"Oh okay!"

Again, that silence.

"I am originally from Chandigarh, and you?", I pushed the conversation again.

"Delhi", she answered looking at her plate. Her expression says that she is not in this café right now, her mind is somewhere far away, and she is sad, like really really sad.

Don't know why, but I have this sudden urge of holding her tightly in my arms, wash away all her sadness and bring back that beautiful smile on her face.

"Is everything okay? Did I say anything that I shouldn't have?", I was somewhat scared.

"Oh no! Absolutely not!", she nods her head. "It's just that.." she paused composing herself. "It's after a really long time, that I am sitting in front of a guy in a place other than my office", she blurted.

Did she just mean that she has not been with someone since a long time? But why? I mean she is a dream date for anyone! There is something which I am missing, something that doesn't allow her to be herself! But no such reason in this world can compensate for her beautiful smile. Will she ever allow someone to know those reasons? And also, I want to jump up with joy after getting to know that I am someone with whom she agreed to meet after a long time! Lot of thoughts started weaving threads in my head.

But back of my mind I just know one thing, she trusted me and agreed to meet by moving out of her comfort zone, and at any cost I won't allow her to repent this decision.

She needs a friend, and I will be that, if she allows me to be one.

"Then I should call myself the luckiest man in this world, I guess!", I tried to make her smile.

She passed a half smile.

Lot of emotions were piling up in my mind at that very second, so finally I gathered some courage and spoke up "Look Misha, I know there is something which is bothering you a lot. I know you don't want to share it with me as you don't have enough trust on me, and I completely understand that. But still if you need a friend to pour your heart out, just know that I am always here. I don't try to make a lot of friends, nor do I try to send my daily updates to irritate someone. I am doing all of these because genuinely I want to be a friend of yours only if you allow me to be one. If you ask me why I want to, seriously speaking I can't cater you with reasons, just that when I saw you for the first time I didn't want that to be our last time. I felt there are lot of untold stories between us, and our journey is a long one! I may sound foolish, but it's fine. Just know one thing, Rishi's friendship is there with you always!", I blurted out everything and took a deep breath.

Misha is staring at me, her blue eyes are moist, and they are saying thousands of words. Swallowing the lump in her throat she said, "I didn't know that Rishi has this philosophical side too, quite impressed I must say!"

"Haha, Rishi has lots of colors to show, just keep watching Miss Grumpy", hearing me she laughed her heart out, and I was happy by seeing her.

I understood that she wants to change the topic and I happily told my mind to do so.

We spoke for another half an hour about my office and her office, how my manager is different from hers, and then I started observing that she is becoming more of herself, she is laughing, smiling and most importantly her eyes are also dancing, they are not trying to be sad as before.

I was delighted.

We finished our food and came out of the café only to find out that it's raining.

Hyderabad and rains have this beautiful relationship where they are always trying to meet each other no matter which part of the year it is. And now being the month of August, their meetings have become way more frequent than before, which is too much for us to bear sometimes!

Misha is trying to book a cab back home, but due to bad weather conditions no cabs are available at this time. I offered her a ride back home, which she refused at first but after me nagging for 5 minutes, she eventually gave in.

I started my car and said to myself, "This day is just getting more beautiful with time!".

Chapter 7

Misha

Everything is appearing to be blur in front of my eyes.

Do my eyes have tears?

No No, I can't cry in front of Rishi. Don't know what's happening with me, a jolt of emotions is running through my mind and it's going to burst out anytime soon. I need to control myself.

"*Misha, just 20 minutes and you will reach home. Don't ruin this drive like a silly girl*!", Mini-me scolded me.

Do you sometime have that sudden urge of spilling out everything that's running at a tremendous speed in your mind? Like you are a volcano right now which might erupt anytime, you never know. This sudden change in my life, meeting Rishi at this café, has brought back all the unresolved pain which I want to throw out. His words in the café regarding if I want to share something with him or not, if I truly trust him as a friend, have caused a huge turbulence in my heart. Right now, I desperately want to share everything with him, cry my heart out and throw out all my pain. There is something in him which is dragging me towards him, and I don't know what really it is.

Beside Shweta, I don't actually have a friend to share my heart with. Shweta is undoubtedly a gem, but I know I can't always bring up my painful thoughts or flashbacks in front of her. She has seen me in my worst time and have helped me a lot to come out of that phase, so I don't want to disappoint her saying that those memories still haunt me, and I have not really able to move on in my life. I know it will upset her, and I don't want that. So, I try to put on a happy face always hiding away my thoughts in one corner of my heart.

But I am tired of hiding, I want to face my demons and overcome them and lead a normal happy life like everyone else. I want to move on.

Right now, I am sitting in this car, but my mind is thousand miles away, and I don't know how to put things together.

I know Rishi is noticing me through his side glances.

I know he is regretting this meeting with all his heart.

But I am helpless. I am suffocated.

Despite the AC of the car being set at 24 degrees temperature and the drizzles outside, I am still perspiring.

"This humidity in Hyderabad is a real pain sometimes, I really hate it!" Rishi's voice disrupted my thoughts.

"Yeah, same here" I struggled replying.

Suddenly Rishi saw something and slowed the car, "Look at those mouthwatering Pakoras man! Let's have it! I love those Chili Pakoras, they are just the best!"

His excitement seeing those Pakoras made me smile. I never saw someone of his age getting excited seeing these little things, he is different. Something is there in him which is dragging me towards him though I am constantly pulling myself away.

"Okay, let's have it, I love them too!"

After hearing my words his smile got broadened and he parked the car at the side of the road.

"You wait in the car, and I will bring the Pakoras here as it is raining outside. Also, will you have tea?"

Something snapped inside me which made me say "No wait, I am also coming with you."

In the last few years, I didn't purposefully go out in the rain though it used to be my fondest memory from childhood days. I loved everything about rains including the smell of the rain-soaked sand. But everything in my life changed years back, and I have secluded myself from rains as it brings back the worst day of my life.

It was a similar rainy day 2.5 years ago when.. "*Misha please, stop going there now. After 2 years suddenly today, you wanted to go outside in rains, so things are turning good, just have faith*!" Mini-me is always more optimistic than me.

I open my seatbelt to get out of the car with Rishi, and I can notice his eyes smiling. He is happy because I insisted on coming out of the car to buy Pakoras.

My heart smiled.

As I stepped outside, drops of rain kissed my eyes and cheeks, and it was like dream walking for me. My legs refused to move forward, and I stood there with my head tilted up towards the sky, allowing myself to relish the taste of rains after so long.

Why did I stop doing this? Why did I close this window of happiness in my life?

Rishi is staring at me with lot of questions and surprise contained in his eyes. He didn't expect to see this side of me.

"Someone enjoys rains, I guess!" he teased.

"Way too much! It's something that brings back all my beautiful memories from childhood, I just love it!" the excitement of my voice was unrecognizable to me too!

"So, you should have said this before, we could have just walked a bit in the rains outside the café before driving back home."

Now, how am I supposed to explain him that this is the first time I came out in rains after 2 long years, though I don't know why but I want to tell him everything.

"Let's just go and order the Pakoras fast, or else your Chili Pakoras will get finished" I just avoided his last question and started walking towards the Pakora stall.

Rishi followed me.

We ordered 2 plates of mix pakoras and 2 extra chili pakoras along with. The aroma of these pakoras have already doubled our hunger. We found two empty stools near the stall, and we sat there. The stools have an umbrella covering it from above, which protected us a bit from the rains.

As our pakoras and tea arrived, we started eating.

Biting one of the chili pakoras, Rishi starts speaking "You know, sometimes me and Varun like to have scooty rides during rains. It's the real fun!"

"Who is Varun?"

"My flatmate, I told you yesterday, you forgot? Rishi's words slapped my memory.

"Oh yes, how can I forget? Your daily update included that scooty ride as well!"

His eyes glistened knowing that I remember.

Yes, I remember every single thing he said in last few days, don't know why but I am getting dragged towards him without having any control whatsoever.

"Yes exactly! So eventually it turns out that you have carefully read all my messages!" Rishi grins.

My cheeks turn red.

"Nothing like that, it's by chance that I have read few of your messages, but most of them was left unread as I didn't have time to go through your stupid updates!" I tried to sound rude so that Rishi's expectations don't rise up.

"Oh, I see!" He passed a lopsided smile.

By reading between the lines, I can clearly say that Rishi knows that I am lying. He knows I have eaten every word of those chats and I remember everything.

Still, I choose to keep my mask on.

"Don't you get bored by staying all alone?" Rishi throws his next question. The one thing that I have clearly discovered about this guy is that it is very difficult for him to choose silence.

Something which I try to avoid in my life. *Or should I say I am scared of?*

"I chose this life for myself, and I am happy with it. I like my me time a lot!" I smile, hiding my eyes full of loneliness.

Rishi narrows his eyes and looks at me, he seems unconvinced.

"But as per my observation, your Instagram feed says the complete opposite story. It's full of travel photos where you have stayed in hostels, with lot of other strangers and made some great friendships and enjoyed every bit of it. So, Misha, don't make me believe that you prefer staying alone, I am not buying that story!" Rishi smirked.

Oh, God save me!

How do this man know so much about me! Whatever he said is just so true! Even he is more confident than mini-me! *"See I told you already.."* before mini me can finish adding the extra scoop of ice cream, I look at Rishi with stern eyes.

"So, you are stalking me way too much now, and I don't really like it!"

Saying this I stand up and walk towards the dustbin for throwing my empty plate and cup.

"Why you always prefer to put on that shitty mask? Trust me it's easier to show your true self than to fake one!" Rishi's deep voice from behind my shoulders gave me cold shivers.

I froze.

It took few seconds to compose myself and then I turn back towards him "Do you actually feel that you are that smart and powerful to walk into my life all of a sudden and start questioning about every inch of it? You know what, I have given you enough of my time and I am already regretting every bit of it. So, if you can just excuse me then I will be more than happy to go back home and never talk with you again!" I throw a hard glance on his face while saying these words.

Yes I need to hurt him, or else I will get hurt again and I won't do that to myself. I need to distance myself from him, because he is trying to enter into a life which is nothing but a lost star. I can't give him false hopes. I need to protect him by letting him go. So, this is the best that I can do.

But strangely Rishi's face is calm after my words. He steps towards me and looks into my eyes and says "How can you hold so much pain in your heart? Why don't you let it go?"

I don't know what happened at that second.

I broke into tears.

Light rains are still falling down which wash away my tears, as I stand in front of Rishi and start crying heavily.

All those emotions which was piling up in my heart, burst out like a volcano.

Rishi didn't stop me from crying. He just held my shoulders with his hands and let me cry, to throw out my pain.

We are standing under this tree, and thankfully there was no one around us to catch this show. The shopkeeper in the stall was busy frying pakoras so he didn't pay any heed towards us. After few minutes when I calmed down, Rishi asked me "Do you want to get back to the car?"

I nodded with moist eyes.

We both went inside the car without saying a single word and sat silently. Rishi fetched a water bottle from the backseat of the car and passed it to me.

"Drink" he said with a sad smile.

I don't know why but something happened inside me which pushed me to say, "Don't you want to know why I cried?"

"I don't want to push you. I know that when you feel it's the right time, you will share it with me." He said with an understanding face.

But for someone like me, caged in her past, the right time will never come. I know that I will carry this burden of thoughts in my mind always. But a voice from the corner of my heart wants to share everything with him now, I want to feel light like a feather, I want to smile.

And he makes me smile.

I gathered all my courage and said, "I want to tell you a story".

The biggest story of my life.

Chapter 8

Misha

3 years back..

"This dress is really pretty Misha, it looks amaaazinggg" Amisha's voice startled me from behind.

I was busy applying lipstick as the final touch to the look. We, the employees of HappyLaughs company are having an office party today evening. We are supposed to directly reach the venue from office, so as usual the girl's washrooms are heavily packed today where everyone is getting ready before the party. Also, can't ignore those mirror selfies in between!

I am also one of them, holding lots of cosmetics in my hand and lots of hopes in my eyes. I have recently shifted to Hyderabad, because of this job and I am pretty excited about it. After applying the lipstick, I look at myself in the mirror. The body-hugging-knee-length black dress is undoubtedly suiting me well. With my high heels and red lipstick, I am feeling super confident today.

Being the senior HR, I have this responsibility of transporting people timely to the venue hanging on my shoulders! So, I quickly give a call to Sneha, a junior of mine in the HR department, *although I always avoid calling her!*

Hi Misha, What's up? Are you ready? Her voice always reminds me of her constantly nagging nature which irritates me a lot. She has this habit of poking her nose into everything happening around her and draw out juicy gossips out of it. I hate gossip, and so, being poles apart, we couldn't be friends despite of working in the same department.

"Yes I am ready. Please send a copy of the roaster to me, and coordinate with first 6 teams and I will do the same for the last 6", I tried to keep the conversation short.

"Oh..but I was planning to coordinate with team 7&8, will that be possible?" Her over dramatic voice itched my ears.

I exactly knew why she was asking this, according to the roaster, Ritika is in team 7 and they both are always gossiping about everything going on in the office, apart from doing actual work.

"No, the list is final, please coordinate accordingly. You can go in any of these first 6 cabs but try to reach the venue by 7.30 PM as we are already running late" I tried sounding strict.

"Fine, will do that, bye" Her voice clearly shows she is pissed off. But who cares?

We are small startup company, with strength of around 90 people. Out of which around 80 are attending today's party, so we have booked 12 cabs as few of them also opted for going to the venue by their own. Accordingly, we divided everyone in teams and allotted them in different cabs.

We reached the venue at 7.45 PM.

The party started with Rajiv, our CEO, announcing few achievements for the last year. I was too astonished to hear my name as the "**Stand Out Performer**" of the year.

It was overwhelming for me.

As I approached towards Rajiv, he handed out the certificate to me and passed a full big smile.

"Congratulations Misha, you truly deserved this! You were amazing!"

I controlled my high beam smile and just shyly passed a smile saying, "Thank You!"

Rajiv has always been extra supportive for me, which I appreciate mostly but sometimes I find it too suffocating. His over friendly nature towards me plants a thread of misconceptions in my colleague's heads, as they feel that he is biased towards me. But deep down I know that every day I need to slog my ass off for making sure that everything is running smoothly.

"Hey congratulations, well deserved!" a not so familiar voice spoke from behind. I turned back to notice a pair of dazzling brown eyes focused on me. *Such pretty eyes, Misha*! Mini-me jumped up.

It took me few seconds to recompose myself and I finally spoke "Oh..Hi Kunal! Thank you so much!" with a sheepish smile.

So, Kunal is a new joiner in our organization, who joined our marketing team few weeks ago. In these few weeks we have hardly met in office, as the Marketing team sits in the last section of our office floor. I guess that's the sole reason of missing out on those pretty eyes! *Also, the goofy smile, Misha!* Mini-me is drooling with me.

Before Kunal could say something, I got surrounded by few of my friends who started to drag me for drinks. I couldn't say "No", *though I desperately wanted to!*

I had a quick eye contact with Kunal before leaving with my friends. His eyes somewhat pleaded me to stay back, and my eyes had heaps of guilt submerged in it.

"Misha, you are not drinking enough!", Shweta said by passing another glass of red wine towards me. Shweta is one of my sweetest friends in the office, and we genuinely vibe together.

I adore her.

I am pretty well aware of the fact that I am not drinking or enjoying properly, as my eyes are constantly searching for Kunal in the crowd. His brown eyes, his tall stout structure and that beautifully trimmed beard!

Everything about him is just like that nectar attracting the bee inside me. And that smile! Oh God! Please someone stop me from staring at him!

I am happily fangirling at this second.

Shweta kept on insisting me, which made me drink 2 glasses of wine in a row and I started feeling dizzy after that. With the music, wine, and Kunal within the reach of my eyes, I was vibing with myself at that very moment. I started dancing with the third glass of wine in my hand.

It was one of the most exciting nights till date.

Suddenly I saw Kunal coming towards me. Those brown eyes were telling me a lot of things. Is this happening for real now? I wanted to pinch myself.

"You are so pretty" was his first few words.

"Will you dance with me?" were the next ones.

My mind was not working properly, and I was way too much happy today. I started dancing with him.

At that very minute, a swarm of butterflies started dancing in my stomach, I was the happiest girl on this planet.

His hands were holding my waist and my hands covering his shoulders. We were swaying through the tunes of the music, and to add that cherry on top, "A thousand years" by Christina Perri is being played in the background. Bringing his lips close to my ears Kunal asked, "Will you have dinner with me tomorrow?"

I blushed and nodded.

We kept dancing silently with the music, and our eyes did the job of our lips. We spoke a thousand words through our eyes which didn't need words to define them. He was holding my waist tightly and occasionally his fingers kept exploring my back. I didn't stop him, as I was enjoying every bit of it. He brought his lips close to my ears again and asked, "Should we have another drink?"

I happily agreed.

We went out of the dancing crowd and moved towards the bar counter. "Red wine right?" he winked.

He was noticing me all this while! Mini-me is dancing on my head right now.

"And scotch with soda for you, right?" He needs to know I was checking on him too!

This little girl is becoming so bold today.

"Stalking me huh?" he asked with a slight brush on my fingers with his thumb.

I shivered. My voice got choked at that moment and I was unable to speak.

I guess my cheeks had the best color shade of blush on them!

"Sir, have your drinks!" the bartender's voice brought me back to my senses.

As soon as Kunal handed me my wine glass, I started gulping it down like a glass of water. "Slow down girl, we have plenty of time in our hands" Kunal was being flirtatious, and I was enjoying it!

Now, after almost 4 glasses of wine in a row, I was pretty drunk, and so was Kunal. We escaped the crowd and stood at a corner, away from the eyes of everyone. I stood in front of him, and he being 6 feet tall, I felt like a child with my 5'2" height!

"We never met actually in office, did we? I just remember your joining day in office and after that it's like you disappeared!" The wine was the one helping me to speak here.

"But I saw you numerous times. The day you were wearing that blue dress in office, I just couldn't take my eyes off you!" Did he just say that he was noticing me since the beginning? Our eyes got locked and we had unspoken thoughts trailing between us. Suddenly Kunal held my hand and pulled me slightly towards him.

I flowed.

With lots of wine running in my head and the dreamy lights of the club, I was lost in that moment. We both kept looking at each other, and my gut instinct told me something was about to happen. Before I could actually find that answer a voice from my back startled me.

"Misha you are here, we are searching you for so long!" Shweta's voice jerked me up from within and it took me few seconds to realize what is happening around me. Kunal has loosened his grip and left my hand. We both turned towards Shweta and tried acting out the best out of us.

"Kunal was just introducing himself, he is a new joiner you know? The one in the marketing team?" I spoke.

"Whatever! Now please can you just check about our returning cabs, as people want to go home, it's pretty late!" As Shweta was pretty drunk too, she didn't pay heed to what was happening between me and Kunal. Thank God!

"Oh, I am so sorry, I didn't keep a track on the time. It's because you forced me to drink too much!" I held her hand and started walking towards the rest of the team members.

"Tomorrow we are meeting at 7PM", Kunal's slow husky voice close to my right ear from the back made me weak in my knees. He left a lingering breath on my bare right shoulder, and I had goosebumps all over my body. "Bye girls let's meet in office tomorrow" he said to both of us before leaving, and of course he didn't forget to wink at me before turning back.

God! This boy is something else!

Somehow, we all managed to safely reach our homes. I will never forget this night in my life.

We met the next day, the day after and the day after that. It was like a ritual. We kissed thousand times a day, and our life was pretty good. We don't meet anywhere outside in Hyderabad, our only meeting place is my flat. It's because he says that he don't want anyone to know about us, as it can go beyond our work ethics, and it can hamper the career for both of us.

I believe him happily.

He says, he loves me more than anything, I believe him.

I love him with everything I have. He is my light, my blessing.

I have started loving this secret cute relationship of us, stealing ourselves from the rest of the world. I have started creating an imaginary world in my head with him, and I am the happiest residing in it.

In office, we rarely talk with each other, though we text throughout the day. I told him one day that Rajiv's behavior towards me is weird, I find him unnecessarily extra sweet, and I don't find it appreciative. He said to ignore everything, as all of these is just in my head. Also, I should feel good to be the one who is in the good books of the CEO.

I believed him again.

He says that his Nani (Grandma) stays alone in Peddapalli, which is around 150 kms from here. His Grandfather died a year ago and his grandma doesn't want to leave back his memories there, so she stays alone. Kunal needs to visit his Nani every weekend to give her company, and so we can't meet on weekends.

I agree happily, again.

Sometimes I ask her to share photos from the weekend, but he says that his Nani hates smartphones and she is allergic to clicking photos. Sometimes he sends random photos from weekend, like his plate of food, or his weird happy selfies and I am contented.

One evening he says "You know Misha, I really want to buy a place in Hyderabad someday and convince my Nani to stay with me for few days in a month. Just imagine, you, me and my Nani enjoying a Sunday afternoon together! It would be so much fun!" Kunal's words added a layer of bricks on my dreams. Does it mean that he is manifesting a future with me? I am happy as lark now!

Caressing my bare back with his long sling fingers, as I lie keeping my head on his bare chest, he continues "But for that, I need to get this promotion soon! The sooner I become the Marketing Manager, the faster I can chase my dreams, I mean "Our dreams" Misha!" I kiss his chest and hug him tightly saying "Don't worry it will happen soon! I will help you in every possible way, don't worry love!" Saying this I take a mental note of having a word with Rajiv regarding the Marketing manager position.

I was so much in love that it felt like my life is on summer vacation. Everything around me was like freshly bloomed flowers and I was glued to their fragrances. I was dancing until that very day, the day which changed everything in my life.

The worst day in my life.

Today is a usual slow-paced Monday. I am in office, scrolling through my phone. Kunal is on leave today, as he extended his stay for a day at his Grandma's place because she is not keeping well since last few days. He will come back tomorrow morning. I am counting down the hours as I am desperately waiting to meet him and hug him tightly in my arms. Also, it may sound cheesy but today marks the completion of 6 months since the day we spoke for the first time in the office party.

Suddenly something strikes my idle mind and I plan a surprise for him. I decide to go to his place after office and slide a letter through the gap beneath his front door, and once he opens his door and enter his flat tomorrow morning, he will be utterly surprised. This idea was obviously stolen from a Bollywood movie, but who cares right?

Planning this surprise made me so happy, I started writing the letter to him, penning down all my emotions. Starting from our first meeting to every little thing we shared, I wrote everything. After pouring my heart out, the letter landed into 5 pages! I neatly folded it and put it into an envelope. Tying a red ribbon around it, I wrote on top -

With all the love in this world,

Yours' Misha

After office, I booked a cab straight to his place. Mostly we meet at my place as he says he loves my place more. I went to his place twice, and I loved it! It's a one BHK apartment which is nice and cozy. As I reach his place, I run towards the elevator and press the button 9 for reaching his floor. My mind is transported to imaginary thoughts where I can see his face glowing with happiness after he reads my letter. Breaking my thoughts, I reach his floor and I walk as fast as I can towards his apartment.

As I bend down to slide my letter under his door, I could hear some footsteps from inside. "It's from the 8th floor I guess" I said to myself and ignored it. As I got up and turned around to go back, I heard Kunal's voice from inside his apartment. "I am coming baby, just give me two minutes!" I heard this line standing outside the door.

My legs froze for few seconds.

I couldn't register what's happening at that moment. My mind started revolving and I ended up moving the latch of the front door with my hand. Surprisingly it opened! I entered his apartment. The drawing room is dark, with only a fade blue lamp throwing some light. I could hear voices coming from the bedroom. For once, my brain and heart both stopped working, and all I wanted was to run away.

But I couldn't.

My body dragged me towards his bedroom. The door was half closed, and a yellow lamp was lit inside. I peeped into the room and my eyes were filled with horror. Kunal and a girl, both naked, lying on the bed and making love.

I wanted to throw up. My head was spinning, and my legs were trembling. My lips were jammed and so was my heart. The only thing that came out from my mouth was "Kunal, how could you?"

Hearing my voice, they both turned towards me in shock. That girl quickly wrapped herself in the bedsheet and Kunal started fumbling. "I can explain this to you, it's nothing as it seems to be, please let me explain!"

I couldn't say anything, I was standing still at that moment.

"Why are you saying sorry to her Kunal? This was bound to happen someday, right? We are together since last 4 years and it was our plan to trap Misha in this web."

While wearing his shorts Kunal said "Stop Simran! It's not the right time to talk about all these, please!"

I am standing still, frozen. My lips have lost their ability to speak and my heart its ability to feel.

With a wicked smile pasted on the lips, Simran continued "But still, I appreciate your acting Kunal! You were great! You made this poor girl believe everything you said. The story of your Grandma and your weekends, how desperately you want to buy a house here, everything was so well planned! And this silly girl believed everything by creating imaginary love stories in her head. God! how come you are so dumb Misha? Do you want to know why we did all these? Because of your fucking CEO Rajiv! He promised a managerial position to him before joining, which he didn't fulfil. And you are the one, Rajiv is always drooling over, so we needed you for our goal baby! You meeting Kunal in the office party and everything that happened after that was a part of our plan! We almost succeeded in it if this wouldn't have happened today. You were about to speak to Rajiv and Kunal would have been promoted with a huge salary hike. Our lives would have been sorted after that, we could have got married easily and started our life together. But you ruined everything!"

At this point, uncontrolled tears started running down my eyes and I could only manage to say one line to Kunal "HOW COULD YOU KUNAL? HOW COULD YOU DO THIS FOR SUCH A SILLY REASON?"

"Listen to me Misha, we both were desperately in need of money, this promotion would have sorted many things in my life, so I was helpless…."

His voice started fading, as my ears started refusing to hear anything after that. I turned back and started running.

Run Misha, Run.

The only voice that ran in my head.

I ran as fast as I can, until my legs gave up.

Standing somewhere in middle of a lonely road, I crashed myself on the road and started crying.

It's raining profusely outside.

I cried my heart out and I couldn't stop. It felt like I am in a dark tunnel, and I don't know the way out from here. Drenched in rains, sitting on the lonely road, I kept crying for hours. Time stopped for me.

It was the biggest nightmare of my life.

The worst day of my life. It changed me. It changed everything.

Chapter 9

Rishi

Imagine yourself sitting on a roller coaster, and suddenly it starts moving in the opposite direction, upside down. You are falling from a height and your heart has stopped working due to fear. Suddenly the roller coaster hits the ground, and you fall apart, breaking your body and your soul. If I could pen down the exact feeling of my heart right now, it somewhat resembled this.

She was sitting in front of me, with swollen red eyes, and I don't know how to comfort her, although I desperately want to!

Me and Misha are sitting in the car since past 2 hours, while she narrated her story. The most horrible incident that can happen to anyone in a lifetime.

After a tough silence of few minutes, I swallowed the remaining balls of tears in my throat and say, "He didn't deserve to breathe the same air as you."

Misha looked at me with her pretty blue eyes filled with tears and looking at those eyes something sparked inside me which made me hold her face with my palms and I whisper, "You are the truly beautiful inside and out, so never ever forget your worth for anyone's sake, you are priceless Misha."

She stares at me with a bit of hope flickering through her eyes, adding a tint of smile on her lips she said "Thank you for listening to my story, it's the first time in the last 2.5 years, I have shared this with anyone. I was tired of piling up bundles of sorrow in my heart and I desperately want to throw them away and move on in life. Every night, I have these nightmares stealing away my sleep, and I hate them to the most. Heartbreaks hurt, but getting deceived by someone you love is the worst feeling ever!" With tears flowing on her cheeks, she speaks without taking a pause.

I look at her, she is different, she is divine.

I am falling hard for her, and I miserably need to control myself. Because right now, it's just about her not about me. I need to bring that smile back on her face and life, and hold her tightly, away from all the sorrows of this poor world.

Because she deserves the best, she deserves the world.

"Is that the reason for you to quit your HR role and join as a Learning & Development specialist?" I look at her eyes.

She shifts her eyes towards the window and says "Yes, that is the reason. I gave my resignation the very next day."

"I swear, I just want to kill that Kunal someday!" I say with deep anger in my voice.

Misha turn towards me and says "It's over Rishi, I don't want to think about him anymore. I just want to throw away that pain out of my body, out of my soul."

Yes, she is right, I will not allow that past to ruin her life anymore, she needs to move ahead in her life. I will bring back that cute smile on her lips and eyes*, just as a friend.*

"I think we need to go back home, it's pretty late already." Her words break my thoughts. I quickly turn by hands towards the steering wheel, and say "Yeah, sure let's go! I will drop you in next 10 minutes" If you ask me then I don't want to leave her for a second away from my sight, but I have to as I need to be that friend for her, whom she can trust with everything.

"We can have dinner together at my place and then you can leave, and we can order something from Swiggy, because my culinary skills are not that good!, sounds good?" With her eyebrows dancing on her forehead, she asks.

Sounds good? Sounds the most amazing plan for me! Spending some extra time with her will always be the best thing on my plate, and right now I am super excited about it.

"It's perfect! I am super hungry too! Let's go fast!" My voice echoed the heavy excitement which for sure was not clearly asked for! I mentally scold myself.

She opens the door of her apartment, and I am clearly in awe with her flat. The place resonates with her personality and without a blink of an eye, I can say that she created this place from the scratch. It's beautiful, minimalist, and classy, just like her. The living area is mostly filled with pastel colors, in contrast with her cushions and paintings which are adding that pop of color in it. I could clearly hear Varun's voice saying "Bro, this is how a house needs to be kept! Stop littering things here and there!"

"Yeah bro, whatever!" I try to kick out Varun from my brain and quickly promise myself to keep my room cleaner than before! This girl has already started bringing magic to my life!

"You have a really beautiful place Misha, you should have been an Interior Designer!" I smile.

She blushed.

"I love rejuvenating my place, as it gives me comfort from the chaos. Keeping my place happy, is like a meditation for me."

"I thought you to be quite a chaotic one! You turned out to be a complete opposite one" I laugh.

Rolling her eyes at me she says, "I might be a grumpy one, but being chaotic is not my genre!"

"Got it, got it, now stop rolling your eyes at me, I am getting pretty scared!" I try to make an innocent face.

She laughs out, her laughter creates waves of music in the air, and I inhale the sound of it.

"Can we order food now? I am dying out of hunger!" she makes a cute puppy face. We sit on her sofa, keeping a safe distance between us. "Will you have Biryani? This place called Potful Biryani serves some amazing Chicken Biryani, I love it!"

Seeing the excitement in her eyes makes me smile.

She is heavenly, she is divine.

"Yes sure, I love Biryani!"

"Look, there is Chicken 65 Biryani, Nati Biryani, and many more options.." she comes close to me with her phone to show the options, and God, my ears refuse to hear any further and my brain stops working for a second. My raging heartbeat is beyond control, and I am completely lost in that moment.

As she comes closer, her hair touches my cheeks, and her elbow touches my chest. The beautiful smell of her hair just pushed that thirst in me of caressing them with my fingers. She is busy showing me the menu, and I am busy saving every detail of her in my heart. I have this sudden urge of pulling her to my chest and hugging her tightly in my arms.

I want to get lost inside her, forever.

"Hey, are you listening? I am ordering Chicken 65 Biryani then?" she turns towards me with her blue eyes. "Yes, that would be lovely" I replied with my fumbled voice.

She shifts back to her place in the sofa and starts scrolling her phone. After few seconds she exclaims "It's ordered, Yaaaay!" I manage to control my laughter, the child within her is the best human on this planet!

"After listening to your story, my respect for you have profusely increased. But, just remember one thing, self-love is always the most valuable thing which you can gift yourself. This is your life, be selfish for once, Misha. You have spent enough time catering to other's needs, it's about time you do something for yourself."

Her eyes grows moist, and she stares at me while I speak. Swallowing the lump in her throat she says "Nobody ever told me something like this! You are a good preacher, Rishi."

"I admit, I am a good preacher! But, I have only selective students to preach though!"

She laughs out hearing me and says, "Glad to know, I am one of them!" Suddenly she falls silent and her expression changes to a serious one, and she continues "But, I genuinely thank you for all the effort you made for bringing me out of my shell. I am happy that I found such an amazing friend in you, and I really treasure our friendship Rishi!"

She stretches out her hand and places her palm on my hand as she finishes her sentence.

Electricity runs through my body.

Remember, she adores the friendship, and she is finally able to trust someone, so don't break her trust by throwing out your feelings. She just needs a friend at this point, and you will be the one for her! My brain made it very clear for my heart.

Hopefully my heart sticks to it!

Looking into her blue eyes and slightly pressing her palm with mine I say, "I feel myself blessed that you trusted me as a friend, and I will never let you down for that, it's my promise."

"Thank you for coming in my life!" These words coming out from that pretty mouth was everything I wanted to hear ever in life.

This day changed everything in my life.

The Biryani arrives and we both serve ourselves.

"It smells so good, Man! I can already say how it tastes."

"See, I told you! This Biryani is everything." Her smile always speaks more than her.

We eat silently while watching some episodes of friends. Or more precisely, she was watching friends while I was busy watching her. The way her nose moves while she laughs, the way she chews her food and occasionally bites her lower lip in between, the way she gulps down coke with tons of ice cubes in it clearly indicates her love for coke, and the way her eyebrows dance while she watches a scene carefully, everything about her is beyond perfect.

She is the most beautiful girl, I have ever met in my life.

Once we finish eating, I go behind her to the kitchen sink to keep our dirty plates. While doing so, accidently her back touches my chest, and for few seconds I start floating in the air. She quickly walks away and starts arranging the remaining things in the kitchen.

"I should get going, it's already pretty late." I say, though my heart has already settled here and will never go back with me.

"Yes, we have offices tomorrow too! You should be going back then." Did her eyes for a second wanted me to stay back longer? *You are overthinking. Her eyes are sleepy, and she wants you to go back, so that she can peacefully sleep!*

My brain is unnecessarily rude sometimes.

I start wearing my shoes, while she says, "It was really nice to meet you Rishi, I will never forget this day!"

"You will not even get a chance to forget it, I will keep on making you remember."

My words make her laugh out loud.

I add to my words "Also, don't miss me much! It's really tough to not miss my presence." I wink at her as I say.

"You wish!, No one is missing you, go now it's pretty late, I need to sleep."

"Okay, goodnight then, miss grumpy!" I give her a sideways hug as I say this.

"Goodnight Rishi, also text me once you reach!" she smiles.

Is she being caring now!

I leave her apartment with a big smile stapled on my lips.

This day has ruined my heart forever. I love her and there is no turning back from here.

Chapter 10

Misha

Should I pinch myself a little more? As, my brain can't actually believe what happened in the last few hours. How come I opened up before someone after so many years and I am actually feeling happy about it? My brain has officially given up on me, *though my heart hasn't.*

"Me, and Rishi are just friends, and we are sticking to this", I try to convince Mini-me while I lock my front door properly and start walking towards the kitchen.

"Don't be a liar Misha, this friendship thing is bullshit!" Convincing Mini-me is never an easy task!

As I reach my kitchen, and start preparing a Chamomile tea for me, my doorbell rings.

Ting Tong, Ting Tong

Who could be at this hour? It's almost 12 AM midnight! I am really scared now.

As I peep out of the eyehole in the front door, I can see Rishi standing there. Oh my God! ! He came back! But for what? Did he forget something?

Did he forget his heart by any chance?

As I open the door, I can see Rishi panting hard. It's obvious that he came back running, so I assume it must be something pretty important!

"Hi Misha, So sorry I bothered you again! But I forgot something."

"You can never bother her!" I wish I could just kill Mini-me someday!

"Oh.. no worries, please come inside and breathe for a second! You are struggling for air man."

"It's completely fine, I just had a quick run from the main gate of your society till here, as the guard refused to give me entry without your permission, and I really wanted to surprise you with something!" He speaks as he began to untie his shoelaces.

I try to control my smile.

"He came running all the way from the main gate, just because of a surprise! Still then you want to call it a friendship, Misha?"

"Yes, it's a friendship and it will be like this forever! Don't dump things in my head!" I scold Mini-me.

"Can I get a glass of water?"

Oh-shit, I should have offered him way before! Such an idiot I am!

"Yes sure, give me a minute" I say, as I fetch a glass from the kitchen and fill it with cold water from the fridge.

He gulps down the glass at one go and takes a deep breath, before opening his mouth to speak.

"Today, I brought something for you, but I forgot to give it in the due course of time. Suddenly I remembered about it while going back, so I thought I should give it today, because 'today' will always be special for me."

I really don't deserve this. How can someone be so kind?

He places a small red box in my hand, neatly tied with white ribbons. I look at him with happy eyes as I untie the ribbons to open the box. My eyes get filled with surprise and delight to find a beautiful magnet depicting a picture of Rohtang Pass, Manali. Though it's really pretty, but I don't understand the significance of it until Rishi starts to speak.

"I was 5 years old when I went for my first trip to Mussoorie, with my parents. While returning from the trip, I was sad and pissed off. I didn't want to come back and was crying like hell on our way back from there. My father stopped our car at a store and bought a cute little magnet written 'I love Mussoorie' on it. He said that I can put this magnet on my book's cupboard and can recall the beautiful memories of this place whenever I want. It somewhat calmed me down and made me happy. Since then, I have collected lots of magnets from each of my travel. These are the biggest treasures in my life, I never share them with anyone. And Rohtang Pass in Manali is the place where I experienced the first snowfall of my life 2 years back, so I collected this magnet to etch that beautiful memory in my heart. I wanted to share something with you, which is really close to my heart, so this is the one! It might sound stupid, but I didn't know anything better than this."

My heart somersaults.

My eyes and heart gets connected at this second, and I can see the most beautiful man on this Earth standing in front of me. Emotions rolls over me, and I tirelessly search for words.

Is it too soon for jumping in his arms and hugging him tightly?

"It's too soon to give away our heart, as we know that it always breaks, right?" I give this final lecture to mini me before I compose myself to face Rishi.

"This is so thoughtful Rishi, something which I never expected in this lifetime. You are becoming one of my best friends now!" I carefully place the magnet on my fridge door as I say this.

"Haha, will be glad to have a grumpy best friend like you in my life; glad you liked my gift."

"I loved it!" I said with a beaming smile. "But I didn't get anything for you, as I was not very sure about how our meet will turn out, I hope you understand" I passed a sad smile.

"Of course, I understand Misha, and you have already ordered the world's most delicious Biryani few hours back, so me and my stomach both have received their gifts!"

Listening to his words, vanished my guilt somehow and made me happy. Whenever he is around me, he makes sure to make me smile and wash away all my worries. *Does love looks like this?*

"I must leave now, it's around 12.30 AM already and we both have work tomorrow! Let me know if you are free in this weekend, we can catch anytime."

Why am I am having butterflies in my stomach with the thought of meeting him again?

"Sure, I will let you know." I tried to hide my smile.

"Also, are we still talking via Instagram, or Can I get your mobile number?" He laughs.

God, you can have my entire world!

"So, you don't want to wait any further, do you?"

"Obviously not! Enough of waiting is already done. Also, I am your best friend from today, so better you give it to me." He rolls his eyes and I laugh.

"Fine, I was just kidding! It's 98757389".

He notes my number in his phone, and I observe him silently. His hair is messy, and the well-trimmed beard adds that extra sharpness to his face. His eyes are dreamy and speaks more than his lips and his fingers are long and sleek, something I can admire for my life.

I am swooning over him, and I should stop.

After saying bye and giving me a sideways hug once more, he leaves. *And he takes a part of me along with!*

I move towards my bedroom with my goofy smile.

Chapter 11

Rishi

I know that I am smiling since last night, after I came back from Misha's place. It's like I am back to my teenage days, and there is a sudden tickling sensation in my stomach, which has permanently decided to settle in my body.

Meeting Misha has made me realize that how you can fall in love with someone so effortlessly. It's like, not falling for her is the hardest thing, but loving her is the easiest thing on this Earth. She is like that line of the novel, which you highlight and read every day to keep your world a happy place. She is that verse of the prayer, which you want to repeat every morning before starting your day, in hope that your day will run well.

But she needs a friend, not a boyfriend.

I tried to avoid all the details to Varun, though I needed to confess some! So, he knows that I met Misha yesterday and we are friends, *as of now!* We didn't get enough time to talk yesterday as it was pretty late, but he has already guessed that my feelings are way beyond friendship. *Did Misha also guess it already?* God, No.. I need to be more careful about my expressions and gestures. I can't just ruin this friendship, I can't let Misha go away from my life. She is my everything.

And now, I am trying to desperately work on a shitty code, but I can't, as my mind is far far away in a beach surrounded by green waters, Misha is walking in the sand and picking up shells. She is wearing a white floral summer dress and her hair is flying with the wind. The wind and sun are teasing her as if they are jealous of her beauty! She is smiling, singing, and dancing! Happiness is oozing out through her eyes. I am sitting on the sand, watching her from a distance and feeling content that I could bring back that smile on her face.

"Stop smiling like an idiot and do some work!" Rohan gives a punch on my back.

"Don't give me lectures, I have already fixed the bug half an hour back!" I snap angrily.

"By the way, who is this girl?" Rohan grinned.

"There is no one, you pretty well know that, stop irritating me and do your work!"

"Are you seeing that girl who came to our office to give training the other day?" Rohan winked with a wicked smile.

God, I just want to dump him somewhere right now! I avoided his question and continued doing my work.

"That girl, because of whom you forced me to have that shitty Pasta?" He continued poking me.

"It's none of your business" I reply frustrated.

"Okay, so it's confirmed now, you are seeing her. She is quite pretty I must say" Rohan passed a heroic smile.

I give up now! It's Rohan, and he will not leave someone unless he hears what he wants to hear from another person.

"It's nothing like that, we are just friends".

"Friendships eventually blooms into relationships" He pats my back. *I hope this too!*

"Stop speculating things for me, and let me work, or else Naveen is going to fire both of us!"

"Bro, he needs us more than we need him! He will never fire us" Rohan smiles turning back to his laptop.

I start working again. I don't want to discuss much about Misha with anyone other than Varun. He is my only friend who is matured and cares about feelings and emotions. Rest are much like Rohan, who are still carrying their teenage brains with them. Misha is a very sensitive topic for me at this moment, and I need to handle it delicately and protect her from the rest of the world. Her smile needs to be intact on her face, no matter how! Never knew I could start loving someone so deeply in just a week!

But she needs a friend, not a boyfriend.

Thinking about her and missing her for the last few hours made me pick up my phone and drop her a text. I am trying not to overstep, so I restrained myself from texting her since morning, but now my emotions are not allowing to handle them!

Me: "Hey, What's up? Busy at work or busy at missing me?:')

Misha: You wish! Just having some soup at home. Not well, down with fever since today morning!

Shit, the Rains!

Me: Oh No! I guess rains didn't suit you yesterday! How is the fever now? Is it better?

Misha: I guess the Rain Gods have blessed me way too much! The fever is not coming down since last few hours.

Suddenly something strikes my mind. She is all alone man! and she is sick! This is not good, and I can't just leave her like that. Cut this bullshit, I need to just go to her. I quickly drop her one more text as I start logging off.

Me: Sorry, my manager is calling for a meeting. Will call you after half an hour, till then try to get some rest. :)

After texting her, I drop another text to Naveen, that I need to leave early today as I am suddenly not feeling well and need to rest. I assure him that I will accomplish the rest of the work from home. As I start packing my things, Rohan notices me and throws a surprise look.

"Hey, you leaving? All okay?"

"Yeah, all good! Just not feeling well, having a terrible headache, will do the rest from home!" I try to act out the best out of me.

"You don't need to worry about work, I will manage that. Go and rest buddy!"

I throw a sigh of relief as he didn't catch my lie.

"Thanks Buddy lets meet tomorrow! It's Saturday, we will enjoy!" I pat his back with a smile before leaving.

I glance at my watch, It's 3.30 PM.

I will reach her place by maximum 4 O'clock.

My heart is beating out of my body, and my nerves are shrinking out of fear as I take long steps towards my car. I know, I am overstepping, and I also know that it can ruin our friendship as a consequence of my desperacy, but still, I choose this option. Because I love her way too much, and I can't leave her all alone when she is not well.

I drive my car as fast as possible and reach her society in next 15 minutes. I am at her doorstep by 3.55 PM. With a racing heartbeat, I pressed the calling bell button.

She opens the door with pale blue eyes filled with surprise as she looks at me.

"Am I hallucinating or is it actually you?

"It's me, Misha. Now if you give me side can I come inside?" I smile.

Misha is still in utter surprise and follows me to her living room holding lots of questions on her face. Ultimately she throws all of them at me!

"How did you come so soon? You were having office right? I spoke with you just half an hour back. Did you leave your work in between? I shouldn't have told you that I am sick!"

"Shh..Shhh.. pause a bit girl, you are forgetting to breathe in between lines! Look, I was just searching for another excuse for meeting you, so I just grasped this one! It always acts as a gamechanger when you come to visit someone who is not doing well, right?" I laugh out loud, to lighten the atmosphere.

But Misha didn't speak a word. She is just looking at me with her blue eyes, holding lots of emotions in them and she wants to bring them all at once on the table.

But I will not force her, until she wills to say something.

"So, how is your fever now?" I ask by placing my palm on her forehead. Gosh! She is having high fever man, she is burning!

"What the hell Misha, your temperature is quite high. When did you have your last medicine?"

"Around 8'0 clock" She said.

"You need to have another one right now. Show me your medicine box."

She silently moves towards her bedroom, and I follow her. She picks up a medicine box from the bedside table and hands it to me. I look for a paracetamol tablet and give it to her. She has it at a go, with her eyes locked with mine speaking thousands of words.

"Now lie down like a good girl. Meanwhile I will make some soupy Maggie for you, it will make you feel better." Saying this, I help her lie down on the bed and pull a soft quilt on her. Her eyes grow moist as she sees me doing all these. I try and ignore it as much as possible, as I don't want to stress her out with any difficult conversation at this second.

"I will come back in few minutes with your Maggie." I smile at her and then turn towards the door for going to the kitchen.

The way she was looking at you was something different today, it's not just friendship. "Don't mess with my brain", I warn my heart.

Thousands of thoughts dance in my mind as I try to concentrate in preparing Maggie for her. I look around her kitchen to find out how neatly she arranges her things everywhere. She attaches these cute labels on each of her containers, specifying the names of the things inside it. Everything is properly arranged without a speck of dust anywhere. Suddenly a realization drools on me, she does all these to fight with her loneliness. She pours all her energy in this flat, to shut herself from the outer world. My eyes grows moist by thinking of it, as I start preparing Maggie for her.

Can I help her to fight in this battle with her own demons?

After 15 minutes, her Maggie got ready. I put the bowl on a tray and carry it to the bedroom.

As I enter the room, I could see Misha sleeping like an angel, with only her face and palms peeping out from the quilt. She is hugging a pillow and resting her chin on it, and she has a tinge of smile on her lips.

I think it's just the appropriate time to kiss her!

I approach her silently and sit on the bed, close to her head. She is turning towards me with her palm resting on the side pillow. I try a lot, but couldn't resist myself, so I end up putting my palm on hers. She readjusts her hand a bit and end up holding my palm. I loved the soft touch of her hand, way too much and I decide not to remove my hand from hers, until she chooses to do it herself. With another hand, I touch her forehead to check her fever. Thank God, the temperature has dropped a lot! I let out a deep sigh. I decide to not wake her up, as she should take rest for few hours, which will help her body to tackle the fever.

Admiring her is my best hobby, I can do it throughout the day. Now with our increased proximity, I could feel her breathe, I could inhale her smell, I could cherish her touch. She keeps holding my hand tightly with her palm, and I keep holding her tightly with my soul.

Suddenly she murmurs under her breath, "I love you Rishi."

My heartbeat stopped for few seconds and my heart came out from my body and hugged me tightly. I repeat those four words in my mind like a prayer.

She is still sleeping, I am still crying.

The Happiest tears of my life.

She said, she loves me!

My soul is shedding happy tears along with me, and I don't know how to express my feelings at this second. "I love you so much, Misha" I whisper under my tears, as I look at her with eyes filled with love.

I keep rubbing my other palm gently on her forehead. Then suddenly my eyes fall on her cute temple, and I start giving gentle strokes with my fingers and take a mental note of kissing that temple someday in my life.

Although she is sleeping, and she is not aware of what she said, but still, I will dream and hope that these four words will be the favorite words of her life.

And today will always be the Happiest day of my life.

She is still holding my palm, and *She said she loves me!*

Chapter 12

Misha

I am strolling in the streets of Paris, scooping out the best days of life, having my favorite croissants and crepes, and enjoying the rays of beautiful European Sun on my bare skin sneaking out from my yellow sundress. My heart is full, my soul is happy. Suddenly a pair of arms with beautiful sleek fingers wrap me from behind, and I instantly know that it's none other than my beautiful Man, my love, Rishi. He kisses my left bare neck, which always happens to be his favorite spot.

Suddenly I could perceive the touch of water on my forehead. It's cold and icy. Is it raining? I look up at the sky….

"Misha, open your eyes Misha, you need to have your medicine" A constant deep voice keeps hammering my mind. I open my eyes after lots of struggle, only to find Rishi is sitting next to my head and hopelessly trying to wake me up.

I was dreaming! But why was Rishi kissing me in my dreams?

"Misha, you are having high fever. I am trying to cold press in a futile attempt to beat the fever since last half an hour. I guess it's time to have another medicine" He says as he keeps caressing my forehead with his fingers.

I managed to say "Okay", with a mumbled voice.

Rishi helps me to get up by throwing his one hand around my shoulders, and tightly holding my palm with his hand. I retire my entire body weight on his hands, as I sit on the bed, resting my head against the headboard. He gives me the medicine and I gulp it down with a glass of water. Weakness rolls over my body.

I realize that my hair is creating a mess, as I have not combed it since last night. So, with my weak trembling hands, I pick up my comb from the bedside table to tame my hair a bit before I lie down again. Rishi's brows are creased with concern as he watches me struggling with the comb. "Let me help you, Misha" He says.

As I don't have any leftover energy to reply, I give in.

He positions me in front of him and sits behind me and starts combing my hair. This feeling is surreal, I have never experienced something so caring and loving before.

"Do you want to tie your hair in a ponytail?" He asks.

I nod softly.

He carefully pulls all my hair to the back and tie it with a scrunchie which was lying on my bedside table. He tries twisting the scrunchie, but it slips between his fingers. I try to hide my smile. "I will do it" I say, as I tie my hair with 2 turns of the scrunchie.

"Why are you doing all these, Rishi?"

"I love caring, especially when it's for you" He whispers.

I remain silent, I remain teary eyed.

"I will make veggie soup for you, till then try to get some rest" He left the room with this line.

Something is different with Rishi today. He is not trying to be that funny, flirting boy anymore. He is showing his caring side, *his loving side.* And strangely it's not making me feel uncomfortable at all. The feeling is so homely, so pure. Him taking care of me or combing my hair, feels as if something which my soul planned far before my body knew about it. It's destined, it's natural.

I am falling for him which was never planned for me in last few years. But if I compare me falling for Kunal and me falling for Rishi, both of them are poles apart. My feeling for Rishi is somewhat how a window feels about the curtains. It's like we both fill in the gaps and complete a sentence, as if he is the noun then I am the adjective and vice versa.

"I told you Misha, true love feels like this!" I don't scold Mini-me today, as I know she is right.

I look at my phone, it's 9.00 PM. I am sleeping since last 5 hours!

He comes back with a bowl of soup and sits beside me. As I try to take the bowl from him, he looks at me with his soft black eyes and says, "Let me feed you, you are too weak now."

I give in with a smile. *Somewhere, I wanted this too!*

He feeds me, with his eyes locked with mine. We speak about thousand things, with unspoken words. Breaking the silence, I say "No one has ever taken care of me like this, thank you Rishi."

He keeps his palm over mine and squeezing it slightly he says "You don't know your worth Misha. You deserve the world, you deserve every drop of happiness falling on your cheeks. So, I am not doing anything unexceptional for you, it's something which you deserve. You are too valuable Misha, don't ever allow anyone to make you feel less worthy."

The words kept echoing in my ears, and I end up hugging him. I hug him tightly with my head pressed against his chest and I cry my heart out. I keep crying and he keeps holding me tightly in his arms, allowing me to bring out all my fears and sorrows. He rubs my back with his hand, while I keep crying. He doesn't ask me to stop. He wants this minute, to be the last minute of pain in my life. He wants a new beginning for me, and I want that too.

After few minutes, I eventually stop crying and sit back. He gives me a glass of lukewarm water, I gulp it down. He starts feeding me again and I deny. "I don't want to have more, please."

"It's not a choice Misha, you need to have it. Your body needs food to fight, so stop being a child." He cutely rolls his eyes. I find it funny.

In the next 10 minutes, my veggie soup gets over and I can see Rishi's contended face seeing my empty bowl. "You should go back now, it's already late" I say.

"I won't leave you in this condition. I will be with you tonight, and don't say No, as I am not going to listen." Before I could say something, he continues "Also, don't worry, I will be sleeping in the other room, and you can be comfortable here. But there needs to be someone around you today, so I can't go back." My heart melts.

"Okay fine, I won't fight on this, but what are you going to have for dinner?" I ask concerned.

"I will order something for me, don't worry" He smiles.

Keeping his palm on my forehead, he continues "The fever has dropped as of now, so you should go to sleep. The more you sleep, the faster you will heal" I listen to him like a child, as he helps me lie on my bed. Throwing the soft quilt on me, he slightly brushes my cheek and says "Goodnight Misha, I am here with you, don't worry."

A wave of relief runs across me, and I suddenly realize what's the comfort of togetherness is. I always tried to guard myself from the world, wearing the amour of bravery and convincing myself that loneliness is a bliss. But today, all of a sudden, my world has turned upside down. I am craving for love, care and pamper. As if my thirsty heart have at last found her bottle of water to quench her thirst.

I deserve to be loved, I deserve to be cared.

Embracing all my courage and fears, I ask him by pointing my finger towards my bookshelf "Can you read that book for me? It will help me to sleep easily."

"Yes of course, thank you for saying out loud about what you want" He says as he picks a romance novel from the bookshelf and sits near my head and starts reading. As he keeps reading, I keep flying in my world of dreams. My heart and head feels light like feather, and I am happy. Yes, I am actually so so happy today.

I used to blame my life for everything in the last few years, but suddenly since yesterday everything has started to make sense. Meeting Rishi, rainfall of yesterday, my fever, all of these was helping me and Rishi to come closer. The Universe conspired in bringing us together, and there is no turning back from here.

"Confess your feelings, Misha! Just tell Rishi, how much you love him" Mini me is jumping in my heart today.

But our feelings are mutual right? Or it's me who is having this feeling, and Rishi just wants to be friends with me? An uncanny fear runs through my spine, as I watch him reading for me.

I decide to wait for somedays before confessing my feelings. These few days will feel like years for me, but I guess it will worth the wait.

"I love you so much, Rishi" I whisper in my heart.

Chapter 13

Rishi

If someone asks me today that how "love" can be defined, I will just smile and say, "Love is when you listen to someone's heartbeat and decode their feelings, it doesn't require strings of words. Beats of their heart is enough to comprehend their soul."

Falling in love with Misha was like falling for myself, it's just like I was searching for the missing part of my life's puzzle and suddenly she came to just complete me. Somewhere deep down my heart, I know she loves me too! I heard it from her while she was sleeping, now I just want to hear from her in her fully conscious state, *it can make me unconscious though!*

It's Saturday morning and I am at her place. Thankfully, she didn't have fever since last night, and she slept peacefully, *while I watched her lovingly.*

I woke up at 8 AM. Actually, I barely slept last night. I frequently checked on Misha at every 2 hours, whether she is having fever or not, also being so close to her, blocked away sleep from my eyes. The first thought that came in my mind after waking up is, I wanted to make breakfast for her. I can just cook for survival, and till date I have never made breakfast in my life! But everything needs to have a first time right?

When you don't know how to cook, then what comes first to your mind? Obviously YouTube! I quickly searched the recipe for a stuffed omelet and in no time my screen got filled with hundreds of mouth savoring recipes. I picked the one which said, "The best stuffed omelet recipe for a beginner", *like me.*

Misha is still sleeping like a baby.

Luckily, I found all the ingredients in her kitchen and fridge. It took me almost an hour to chop the vegetables, mushrooms, and chicken. But finally, I made it. Now lies the main part of the story, frying the omelet! I have never fried something before, and omelet needs to be given a particular form and you need to flip it in a frying pan. It sounded more difficult than attempting questions for CAT exam! But I wanted to try it for her, and so I jumped in the act.

After about 45 minutes and 4 failed attempts, finally I made a not so perfect omelet but still my heart approved it!

Simultaneously, I prepared some green tea for her, and laid all of them together on a tray. It's 11 AM now, I went to the bedroom to wake her up.

I touched her forehead and found it to be cold, which helped me breathe a sigh of relief. Keeping my hand on her forehead I called her gently, "Good Morning, Misha! Wake up, it's 11 AM. You need to have your medicine too."

She peeped out through her one half-eye and said "Why are you here? Why didn't you go back?"

This girl is just incredible!

"I will go back after some time. Now can you please wake up?"

After struggling a bit, she finally sits on the bed. I keep admiring her morning face, it's the best thing I ever saw in my life! Her messy hair, puffed eyes and those cute lips. Everything looked more beautiful than before. How my life would be if I get a chance to wake up to this beautiful face every day of my life? Imagining this, a chill of shiver ran through my spine. Bringing the tray in front of her with a broad smile pasted on my lips, I said "Look, I tried making something for you, hopefully you will like it!" and hesitantly I continued "Also it's my first attempt of making an omelet, so please don't expect something extraordinarily delicious."

Now I am waiting for her expression to change into happiness and excitement.

But the opposite happened!

She looked at me with her puffed eyes, full of tears and suddenly she bursts out in anger!

"I know, I may sound miserable to you but that doesn't give you the authority to sympathize with my life! Stop making me feel more horrible, I don't like all these unnecessary bandages on my wound which will eventually fall off!"

Seeing her loose her temper, made me lose my calm too. I least expected this reaction from her, and witnessing this behavior made me feel like shit. Shouting at the top of my voice, I exclaimed "Nobody gave you the permission to judge someone's intentions in the way you like. If I had to sympathize with your situation then I wouldn't have spent all my time since yesterday taking care of you. Why are you pretending as if you don't understand anything?"

She is silent.

She stares at me with her blue eyes for few seconds and then diverts her attention back to the omelet and starts nibbling it with the fork.

"For God's sake, say something Misha" I screamed.

She remains silent.

I drop all my logical thinking skills out of my head and grab her face with my hands. Tilting her face at an angle to lock my eyes with hers, I said "Don't you really get why I am doing all these for you?"

With her eyes filled with tears, she says "I need to hear it from you Rishi, as I have this fear of trusting someone's feelings for me."

My brows pinch together. How did I not understand this before? Misha needs to be told how loved and wanted she is, to wash away all her insecurities. For someone, who got deceived by trusting and loving somebody, needs this reassurance over and over again. I need to bring back her belief in love, and I will do that at any cost. I also understand one more thing that I can't wait any longer. The more I wait, the more insecurities and negative thoughts will pile up in her mind.

She needs to be told, how much I love her, and this second is the best second for it.

Cupping her face, I look into her eyes with my heartbeats floating on my pupil. Collecting all the emotions which is piling up in my heart since last few days, I say "Misha, I love you, I love you a lot. I don't know, when and how my feelings became this strong, but I just know one thing that seeing you smile makes my world a happier place. For the first time in my life, my heart, body, and brain agreed together without a fight, and I knew at that very second that falling in love with you was the best thing happening in my life."

Tears starts rolling down her eyes as she keeps looking at me.

We both are crying.

I am waiting for her to say something.

My heart is elated. It's clapping and cheering for me.

My brain is still waiting for her to say something.

Chapter 14

Misha

My heart is smiling in a shape of rainbow right now.

A rainbow is formed in the sky, when the sun rises after rains, when the black clouds disappear, and white clouds cover the sky. It's the same way my heart is feeling at this very moment. A new sun of hopes and love is rising inside me, conquering all the black clouds of mistrust and loneliness. My heart is that flower bud now, which is waiting to bloom once again to display all its colors and emotions.

Rishi's confession made my heart stop for few seconds. It was tired of running at a fast pace since last few years due to haunting memories and pain, and now all of a sudden, these words of him stopped my beats for a bit. Calmness rolled inside my body, and I felt light like a feather shedding away all my baggage from the past. I knew he loved me since the beginning, and I loved him too but still this reassurance was somehow necessary for my wounded soul.

I know he is waiting for me to say something, but my tongue is unable to roll words and my eyes are unable to hold the emotions.

I tried to compose myself.

Looking at my beautiful man and holding his face with my palms, I said "Loving you is the holiest thing that I have done in my life. I tried a lot to hold myself back from you but at the end of the day my brain had to surrender before my heart. Before you entered my life, it was full of jumbled words and now you have created meaningful sentences out of them. You pulled me out from my darkness and gave me a new meaning to life. I love you Rishi, I love you more than anything."

Tears are flowing through his eyes as he stares at me.

I continue "Just remember, I am giving you a very delicate heart, keep it safely with you and never break it again. Because it will not be able to endure the pain this time".

With tears covering the words Rishi says "No matter what happens from now on, just remember your heart is in the safest place on this planet. I love you, and this will always be the biggest truth of my life."

I couldn't resist anymore. I throw myself in his chest as his arms wrap me from behind. I keep my head on his chest, with my ears pressed against his heart. I could hear his beats calling my name, I could feel my presence inside him. He keeps holding me tightly in his arms and his chin pressed against my back.

After lots of happy minutes Rishi whispers in my ear "I didn't know making an omelet will turn out to be such a wise decision".

I giggle.

Locking my eyes with his, I say "This will always be the best morning of my life."

Dragging me closer to him he whispers close to my lips with his deep voice "Then let's make this morning more memorable." My knees tremble as he looks at me and before I could say something, Rishi presses his lips against mine.

He kisses me as if I am his first kiss.

He kisses me as if I am his last kiss.

His lips are soft and warm, and they taste divine. Feeling empowers as we continue kissing each other with all our love in our hearts. It's the best kiss of my life till now. Don't know for how long we kept kissing each other, until the ringing of the doorbell brought us back to our senses. Pushing him away, I said "Let me open the door, someone is there outside. I guess it's Ritu Didi, my cook."

"Your cook came at the most perfect time, I must say" Rishi lets out a big sigh.

"Coming back in 10 minutes" I say before I run towards my door to open it.

I have asked both Ritu and Meeru Didi to come late on Saturdays and Sundays, as I love to have lazy late mornings on weekends. Meeru Didi comes at around 2PM on weekends, so this must be Ritu didi.

As I open the door, Ritu didi enters with a smile.

“Misha, how are you doing today? How is your fever?”

“Now, I am much better. Just having cold which will wear off in few days” I smile back.

I enter the kitchen following her, and we both stand still for few seconds with our eyes filled with horror!

The kitchen is looking like our Chemistry lab from school, after a hectic day of experiments! The entire kitchen is filled with different containers, spoons, eggs remnants, spilled sauces and what not. Ritu Didi looks at me and says, “Misha did you bring a new cat or dog pet to your flat?”

I try to control my smile.

“I was experimenting a new dish today morning, for one of my friends. Don’t worry I will clean it now!”

I try avoiding eye contact with her as I go inside the kitchen and start arranging the stuff.

“Don’t fool me Mishu, I know you can’t tolerate the biscuit jars to be changing their position from left to right side, and you want me to believe that all this mess is created by you!” Ritu Didi grins.

I blush.

Surprisingly the clean freak Misha is not at all angry or disappointed today. My fears have washed off and so my shield too. I used to do all these to keep my life protected from the world, but I don't need that any longer.

It's okay to be messy sometimes, isn't it?

"Ritu didi, can you make those mouthwatering Aloo Parathas today? One of my friends is here to visit me, so we both will have lunch together." I say this without looking at Didi, as she very well knows that other than Shweta I have never told her to make Aloo Parathas for anyone else!

"Is he here?" Ritu didi asks with a grin.

"Whom are you talking about?" I ask, surprised.

"The one because of whom I can see my Mishu so happy for the first time in last 3 years."

"Mishu" is Ritu didi's love language.

Ritu Didi is working here since the time I moved to this place. She knows me very well, although she never asks anything. She has seen me before and after the Kunal's phase in my life. So somewhere down her heart she knows how that incident has drastically changed me. She has never questioned me anything regarding it, but has taken care of me silently, and loved me always. So, it's not surprising for me that she understood the reason behind my smile today.

"Make the Aloo parathas fast, I am starving!" I said as I looked at her with my red cheeks.

"It means, today's friend is really special!" Ritu didi winks at me and turns towards the gas stove to resume cooking.

I silently move out from the kitchen with my blushing smile.

As I enter the bedroom, I couldn't find Rishi on bed. I understood he must be in the washroom. I could see that he has tried folding my quilts and making my bed, though it's not folded perfectly. These cute efforts melt my heart every time.

As he comes out from washroom, I jump into his arms once again. He smiles and holds me tightly. Gathering all my courage, I ask him "Can we go out today? Like for a movie?"

I never went on a real date in Hyderabad till now. So, this thirst of walking in the streets of Hyderabad with someone beside me, is indeed very real.

Rishi holds my hands and pulls closer to him. Tucking few strands of hair behind my ears, he says "Are you sure that you want to go out today? You need to rest for at least a day."

Before he could add something more, I put my finger on his lips and announce "We are going out today. I am completely fine, and today is very special so it needs to be celebrated!"

Rishi's eyes glistened.

"Get ready in next 30 minutes. I will show you Hyderabad today!" he exclaims in excitement.

Giving him a peck on his cheek I say "That's like my man! I will quickly take a bath and by then Ritu Didi will make the parathas. We will have them and then start our journey for the day!"

The excitement in my voice was unrecognizable to me too!

"Okay go, but don't forget to switch on the geyser. Don't take shower in cold water or else you may catch cold again."

My over caring Man.

"Sure sir, I will do that." I smile.

"Let me know once you are done, I am waiting in the other room" he says with an understanding smile.

This is the best part about Rishi, he is taking things slowly. He is not rushing in this relationship as he feels that things can get uncomfortable for me. He is a parcel filled with care and understanding, I adore this quality of him.

Before leaving the room, he quickly gives a peck on my cheek.

I blush.

After he left, I open my wardrobe to decide today's wear. I wanted to look pretty and warm today, something which the true Misha loves. I pick a blue knee length summer dress, with white floral motifs on it. I bought this dress few months back and was preserving it for some special day. I found it perfect for today. As I start preparing for the shower, I remember the way Rishi's lips tasted.

It's better than my favorite blueberry ice-cream too!

Misha, can we stop having such weird comparisons! Mini-me made me blush.

Let's jump together in the sea of happiness today! Mini-me shouted, and I happily joined her.

Chapter 15

Rishi

The kiss left an intoxicating effect on my body, which made my heart and mind freeze for few minutes. She said she loves me, and this time for real.

I am still pinching myself every second, because it's a lot for my brain and heart to capture for the day. The feeling of your love getting reciprocated, is just surreal. It's like, I have won the world with her beside me. The way her body fitted against mine was as if we were carved by the almighty only for one another, and the way her lips melted against mine was as if the waves of ocean finally crashed at the shore, it's final and only destination.

It's divine, it's pure.

It's everything.

I want every last drop of her embedded inside me, but I don't want to run things. She has shielded herself for 2 years and finally shedding off all the insecurities, and bringing her true self out of the nut will be tough for her. So, I want to give her all the time in the world, as I know that I will be loving only her for this lifetime and beyond. I want her to feel loved, to feel secured. I don't want her mind to have a speck of doubt on her decision of trusting my presence, and for that I will do anything and everything.

I have texted Varun yesterday that I will not come back home, as I am stuck at Rohan's place for some work. He replied with one word "Okay" which clearly indicates that he knows that I am lying. But it's fine, as I want to narrate him the entire story face to face once I meet him tonight.

She wants to go out with me. Somewhere deep down my heart I know this is her first time of going out in Hyderabad with someone by her side. I want to make this profusely special and for that I have thought about something. Sitting in the other room while she is getting ready, I quickly chalked out a plan for the day. I know she will love the itinerary and I want to photograph that beautiful smile on her face when she will be happy and surprised.

"Hi, I am ready!" a soft voice made me look up from my phone. Seeing her standing in front of me, skipped my beats. She is looking extraordinarily beautiful today. With that pretty white dress, slightly damped hair and that glam on her face. Her blue eyes is always adding that extra shade of beauty, along with her soft moist lips with a tinge of pink gloss on it. Suddenly I have that urge of pulling her to me, digging my fingers in her damp hair and eating the most beautiful lips on this earth! But I controlled myself.

"You are looking divine" I managed to say, with my mouth opened with amazement.

"Thanks" She blushed.

"Come here" I said pulling her hands slightly towards me. I made her sit on my lap and held her tightly with my arms. Slightly brushing her cheeks with my fingers, I continued "You are the most beautiful girl inside and out, on this planet. Loving you is perhaps the most sacred thing that I have ever done in my life."

She wrapped her arms around my neck and said with some smile sparkling in her eyes "I am blessed, that I met you Rishi. You make me the happiest, always!" Saying this she pinned her lips against mine.

I flowed in the land of dreams.

Her lips are soft like balls of cotton, and I loose hold of myself inside them. With my eyes closed, I felt every cell of my body calling her name, and my heart swelled with love.

After few seconds, she eased herself and opened her eyes.

"This lip gloss is addictive! Can I have some in the desert too"? I winked and she laughed.

"Come let's have the parathas, we are getting late!" She gets up from my lap and adjusts her dress.

With creases on her forehead, she continued "And by the way, where are we going today?"

"Umm, it's a surprise and I am confident enough that you will love it!"

Her eyes glistened.

"Okay, then let's go fast. I can't wait any longer."

Her excitement elevated my happiness levels, and I took a mental note of turning this day to one of the most memorable days in her life.

We started our day at around 1 PM.

Weather is pretty good today, considering the rainfalls in past few days the temperature is lower than usual. So, this added some bonus points to our day.

I am taking her first to Shilparamam, which is near Hitech city. It's arts and crafts village which creates an environment for the preservation of the heritage of India. It hosts beautiful traditional and Indian crafts. When I entered Misha's flat for the first time, I have observed the beautiful artifacts and vintage items peeping out from every corner. She loves art, and I can vouch on that. A beautiful handicraft's Utsav is going on, and I know she will love it. I never came here before, but Varun has come here with few of his office colleagues and has showed me pictures of this place. It's beautiful, I must say, and I am excited to show her. *I am just guessing that she didn't come here before too!*

As we were reaching our destination, Misha exclaimed with her excited tone "Rishi, are we going to Shilparamam?"

"Yes baby, we are. Do you like it?"

"I love it Rishi. I always wanted to come here, but Shweta is not very interested in handicrafts and all, so she never agreed. I didn't want to come alone, so it never happened. I am so excited that we came here today. Yaaaay!"

Seeing her this happy, grew my eyes moist.

I just want that smile to be stapled in her lips forever.

We went inside the village, and I must say the place was truly magical. We started exploring different art museums, and Misha was so keen to know about everything in detail. Her interest towards arts and handicrafts is truly commendable. There were also some performances by some wonderful artists showcasing the true heritage of India. We sat and saw few of them, and we loved them. Also, Misha wanted to buy some handicraft items for decorating her home, so we went to visit the stalls. There were numerous stalls showcasing handloom and jute products, hand embroidery wears, and lots more.

"Look at those blue potteries and terracotta things. Let's go there!"

Misha dragged me to those stalls, and I was so happy seeing her this excited. She was busy selecting some terracotta items and my eyes fell on the stall next to it. It had beautiful, handcrafted jewelries and I saw a pair of earrings with blue and white beads on it. I instantly fell in love with it, imagining my Misha wearing them. I quickly went to that stall and bought them. Seeing me coming out from the jewelry stall, popped her eyeballs out from her socket.

I went near her with a broad smile on my face and said, "I have got something for you, as a small token of our first date." As I put those earrings on her palm, her eyes shined like stars. Her lips grew a big smile and she finally said "These are so so pretty Rishi, I love them! Thank you so much." Saying this she started replacing her existing earrings with these. I felt so happy and contented. For the first time, I am having these feelings with someone and it's godly and surreal.

"See, how am I looking?" She asked with twinkling eyes.

I looked at her in awe and said, "Just like a Goddess."

Come let's take a photograph, she said and angled her phone for a selfie. I put my hand around her shoulders and with her cheek resting on mine, we clicked few photos. *I want to frame them for lifetime.*

"I have something for you too" she whispered with a smile.

Saying that she placed a topaz blue colored ceramic coffee mug on my hand.

"It's so lovely, Misha! I love it. Thank you so much!"

"Really? I am so glad that you like it" She gave a soft smile.

"Now this will be my everyday coffee mug" I smile, and she bursts into laughter hearing this.

"You and your cheesy lines, Rishi!"

"Get used to it, because I am going to throw such lines always." I say by wrapping my hand around her shoulder.

She blushes.

After strolling through few more stalls, we finally reach the food court. It's 4.30 PM and we are super hungry by now. After ordering, our food arrived by 5PM. We ate Pav Bhaji and Samosa Chat along with 2 cups of tea. We chatted a lot while eating, regarding our work, her solo travel stories, and lots more. We finished our food by almost 6 PM.

"So, are we heading towards home?" Misha asks.

"Absolutely not, I have one more surprise for you!" I smile.

She blinks her eyes in joy. "Really! Let's go then!"

She holds my hand and electricity runs inside me. We reach to the car, and I press my foot on the accelerator, for our next destination.

This one is a really special one for her, and also for me. While she was showing me her phone the other day while ordering Biryani for the dinner, I accidently saw her Spotify album which was filled with Prateek Kuhad Music. Also, I heard her humming few songs of Kuhad last night. Instantly I knew that she loved his music, and so do I. I loved Kuhad's songs a lot and always looked forward to attending his concerts. Few days before, I came across a post that said, Prateek Kuhad's live concert to be happening today, 26th of August. This coincidence felt magical for me when Misha asked to go out with me today. I quickly browsed through and found only 4 tickets are remaining. I booked 2 of them and was waiting since then for the clock to tick 7PM, for his show commencement.

As I reach the Heart Coffee Café, her brows were pinched together, and she had thousands of questions in her eyes.

“Come let’s go” I said by holding her hand.

“So, are we having a coffee date?”

“Ummhmm..” I nodded.

“Ohh, that’s great!” She smiled, clearly not very amazed.

I smiled under my breath.

It’s 6.45 PM. The show is about to start in next 15 minutes.

As we reach inside the café, a big poster having Prateek’s photo on it can be seen kept on a stand.

She sees it and then stands still for few seconds. Turning towards me with her eyes filled with water she says, “Are we attending The Prateek Kuhad’s concert?”

“Yes we are Misha, this was the surprise for you!”

“I love you so much! This is the best surprise ever! Oh my God, I still can’t believe that I can finally see him performing before my eyes! You are the best Rishi.”

I kept admiring her smile, as she kept saying how excited she is.

This is the smile I live for.

I will do everything for this smile.

Chapter 16

Misha

When I feel cold
I'll keep you close
And if I could hold you
And take you home..

Kuhad is singing these lines, standing in front of me.

Does life really look like this? Or am I in a beautiful dream and once I wake up every inch of my body will ache to sleep back again? I pinched myself again and again, only to reassure my soul that I deserve this happiness, I deserve this love.

Rishi is sitting beside me, humming the lines with Prateek with that addictive smile on his face. I look at him and instantly count my blessings. I mentally declare myself as "God's favorite child" for sending Rishi to my life. Intertwining my fingers with his, I rest my head on his shoulder and whisper under my breath "*Thank you for coming in my life.*"

He wraps his arm around my back and slowly kisses my temple.

Weakness runs through my stomach and knees.

Kuhad continues singing….

My days they begin with your name And nights end with your breath..

This day needs to be the most beautiful day in my life till date. I have madly and completely fallen in love with Rishi, and there is no turning back from here.

With few more kisses and dinner at a beautiful restaurant, our day finally comes to an end. Before dropping me home, Rishi hugs me tightly and whispers in my ear "Dream about me, until we meet again tomorrow!" and gently kisses my bare shoulder with his wet lips. Then he moves his fingers around my neck and throat. Pushing my head back with his palms, he kisses my throat and starts moving his lips down. My legs starts trembling, and a slow moan escapes my lips. I dig my fingers in his back as he keeps kissing me. As his lips touches the hem of my dress, he stops himself and loosens his grip from my body. We both look at each other for few seconds, with lot of untold emotions holding our eyes.

Giving a peck on his cheek, I whisper in his ear "Let's meet in dreams today, until then Goodbye!"

"I am already in my dreams! Bye baby, I love you" He says with a sexy smile.

My stomach churns.

I get down from his car and walk towards my apartment. Before entering my block, I turn back to only see that Rishi is still waiting at the gate. I wave him a goodbye before disappearing from his sight.

Today was something else, Today was really the best day! *Stop blushing Misha, you are red like a tomato!* Mini-me is never tired of pulling my legs!

Sharing every detail with Shweta, is the first thing to be done right now. So instead of going to my flat, I take a turn towards Shweta's home. I am longing to throw up everything before her, and I know she will be really happy for me. *Also, a bit scared maybe?*

I quickly dial her number before pressing the calling bell, as it's around 12 AM and Aunty might be asleep. She picks up in 2 rings.

"Hey Misha, everything okay?"

"Can you open your front door? I am outside" I declare.

"Whatt! Now you are scaring the shit out of me!" She opens the door in a rush and looks at me with big round eyes.

"Relax sweetheart, nothing has happened to me. I just have some really happy news to share with you, so I couldn't resist myself from coming here at this hour."

With a full moon smile Shweta asked, "Please say that you are in love, I am dying to hear it."

Pushing her, I come inside her flat and announce with pride "I have finally found someone, Shweta and I am completely in love."

She hugs me tightly and says “Yaaaay! My ears were dying to hear this from you! I want to hear every inch of the story now. Let me pour us some wine and cheese popcorn before we hop into the bed!”

Snuggling under the AC quilt for next 2 hours, I narrate the entire story to Shweta. Starting from Monday, when I first met him to today, Saturday, how life has completely turned upside down. While narrating, I realized that it’s just 5 days since I first met him. Was it too soon for me to fall in love with someone? But why my brain’s calculations are different from my heart this time? It’s 5 days logically, but my heart is calculating it as 5 years!

Looking at me with big shining eyes, Shweta eats up every word of my story.

“God Misha, Rishi is such a sweetheart!”

“I know, right? Once you meet him, you will like him more.” I smile proudly.

“I am dying to meet him. I want to know who this charming prince is, to steal my best friend’s heart.”

“But Shweta I want to ask you something” I press my lips.

“Now what’s new frying in your head, Misha?”

Embracing all my doubts, I ultimately throw the question running in my head since last few hours “Are things happening too fast with Rishi? Should I need to slow down?”

Holding my shoulders with her hands, Shweta smiles.

"Look Misha, probably I am the only one who has witnessed everything happening in your life since last few years. I have seen you pushing yourself in your shell day by day, and there was nothing I could do to make you feel better. I forgot how your genuine beautiful smile used to be, as you always used to fake a stupid emotionless smile on your face."

She sits up and throws a pillow on her lap. Resting her head on the headboard she continues "I have also seen lots of boys running behind you trying to impress you with their never-ending skills, but you never threw any heed towards them. When I asked you for reasons, you used to say that your instinct says that something is not right. Now, answer me Misha, what happened this time? Why did you suddenly choose Rishi? What was so different?"

"It felt right, it felt so very right with him. He understands me, cares for me and most importantly teaches me to be unapologetically myself. He makes efforts to make me happy and he reads my soul, the inner me" I speak without a single breath.

"You yourself gave all the answers, you were seeking for" Shweta says with a large smile.

Confessing my feelings in front of my brain, made me so happy. Now, I understood it doesn't matter how long a person is with you, what actually matters is how the other person is making you feel. If your heart is reacting well and your smile is touching the sky, then you are in love!

"Thank you Shweta, I feel much lighter than before."

"Thank you won't work! Rishi and you must give me a big fat treat in a good 5-star restaurant soon!" Shweta beams.

"Deal" I smile.

"Also, girl, who on Earth takes his girlfriend to Prateek Kuhad's concert on first date? How come you became so lucky? I am damn jealous now!" Shweta's words brings back the proud smile on my face.

"I have found the best Man on this Earth!" I whisper with a smile.

Passing a big yawn, Shweta says "Let's sleep now, it's pretty late."

I turn to the other side and pull the bedsheets to cover my head. As I close my eyes and try to sleep, my phone vibrates with a message.

I look at my phone with a half eye.

It's Rishi.

Rishi: "I know you are still thinking about me, like I am thinking about you".

My cheeks burn up.

I reduce the light of my screen, so that Shweta doesn't wake up.

Me: "You are disturbing my sleep right now, I was sleeping peacefully!"

Rishi: "How can you sleep peacefully without me?"

My knees trembles.

Me: "My dreams happens to be helping me".

I can see Rishi typing…

Typing..

Rishi: "This day will be forever etched in my memory as the most beautiful day in my life. I am so blessed to have found you, Misha. I love you so much!"

Me: "Love you more baby and thank you so much for today. I have never ever felt so happy in my life."

Rishi: "Anything for that beautiful smile. Also, I spoke with Varun today about us, he is really happy for me."

I smile.

Me "I spoke with Shweta too, she is very excited to meet you! By the way, I am at her place now. It was getting pretty late, so I decided for a stay over."

Rishi: "That's nice, you took a good call :)"

My eyes starts burning and I feel sleepy.

Me: "I am feeling sleepy, can we talk tomorrow?"

Rishi: "Yes sure baby, you should take some rest now. Let's meet tomorrow, till then catch you in dreams! Goodnight Misha, love you."

The idea of meeting him again tomorrow, gave me goosebumps.

Me: "Goodnight Rishi, Love you."

I keep back my phone in the side table and look at the time.

It's 3 AM.

Thank God, it's Sunday tomorrow.

I quickly glide under the sheets and close my eyes. I could imagine Rishi cuddling me tightly and his fingers running across my body. Happiness runs through my veins as sleep takes over me.

I will have the best dreams tonight. *Let's go for it!* Mini me shouted.

Chapter 17

Rishi

6 months later

"Can you pass me the towel please"? Misha's voice jingled from the washroom.

It's 7PM Friday evening and I am at Misha's place.

Sometimes I forget that I am staying with Misha in her flat since last 4 months. Life has been the most beautiful version of it in these months.

Life is twinkling with happiness and our love for each other is growing day by day. Me, Misha, Varun, and Shweta have gelled up really well. We have a common WhatsApp group where we are constantly updating our day-to-day activities. I have this mild intuition that Varun has a crush on Shweta. Although, he won't admit it on his own, but I have shared this with Misha, and she is pretty excited with the whole scenario. "My best friend and yours, dating each other! Just imagine the story Rishi, it would be so much fun" I controlled my laughter seeing her excited face.

Varun is staying alone and has refused to have a flatmate as of now. He needs his place to be spotless, so having a flatmate is like adding thrones to a bed of rose!

I told my Mom and Dad about Misha while I visited home 2 months ago, and their happiness had no bounds. They saw few pictures of us together, and they were ecstatically happy. My mom added that extra footnote saying, "I never knew that such a beautiful girl can say yes to you!" I had only one reply to give which was, "Thanks Mom for being so sweet!"

Misha spoke with my folks too during my stay, and my mom and Misha instantly became friends on the grounds of slagging about me. I just needed a burrow to hide my face! My mom and Misha are now WhatsApp friends where they apparently discuss about their secret skincare and diet plans!

Misha has also shared about me with her parents, and they are happy too. None of us have spoken about marriage yet, though I dream about it every day! I want to give Misha some more time before I ask her hand for marriage. She is coming out of her shell day by day and shedding away all her baggage and I am really proud of her. My respect for her has multiplied in folds and her smile still remains the prettiest thing on this Earth.

4 months ago, Misha suddenly dropped a bomb! "Let's stay together Rishi."

I jumped up in joy as I was waiting for this since day 1. I agreed in blink of an eye, and I shifted to her place in next few days. I am learning to keep the home clean, and Varun is the happiest one seeing my progress. "At least Misha is able to bring some positive changes in you!"

Honestly, not some but a lot of changes have popped in my life with Misha. I have learnt how to speak without words, I know how one needs to constantly love and care for the beautiful heart that's given to him with lots of trust.

It was a month after we started dating when we first made love. It was and will be the fondest memory of my lifetime.

I still clearly remember, it was 24th September, Friday.

We had dinner at a beautiful café, and then suddenly it started raining heavily. While dropping Misha, I also went with her to her flat as I had to pick my Laptop which I left here after work. Completely drenched in rain, we both went inside. Misha gave one of my spare t-shirts that I always used to have in her flat. We both quickly changed in different rooms and then I picked up my laptop and went to Misha to say Goodnight.

"Goodnight baby let's meet tomorrow" I said hugging her.

Suddenly there was a huge thunderclap and Misha dug her fingers in my back and trembled. Then she whispered in my ears "Can you be with me tonight?, I need you."

I shivered.

I looked into her deep blue eyes and my heart skipped few beats. We were standing near her bed, and I slowly removed few strands of hair falling on her forehead and stapled my lips with hers. Her lips were cold and tender that night. We kept kissing as we sat on the bed. She was wearing a light pink colored knee-length nightdress, and she was looking insanely pretty and sexy. I kept kissing her as my hand went to her thighs beneath her dress. I could feel her soft skin which is softer than feathers. I kept kissing her and moving my hand upwards along her thighs. She was trembling and a slow moan tried to escape her lips.

I paused kissing for a second and whispered in her mouth "Tell me when you want me to stop."

"I don't want you to stop, I am all yours Rishi."

My heart smiled hearing this and I gently threw her in the bed. Removing her clothes, I could see her warm skin glowing in the dim yellow nightlamp. I kissed every inch of her body as she kept uttering the four words "Rishi, please don't stop*". I want to play this now as my daily anthem!* Then, we made gentle love where our bodies and souls became one. With the burbling of raindrops and roaring thunders, we kept making love.

It was around 3 AM, as our tired bodies retired to the bed. Misha kept her head on my bare chest and wrapped her arm around my body. I kept running my lazy fingers in her hair, as she gently threw out her most honest fear.

"Rishi, you won't leave me right?"

I knew somewhere deep down her heart, she holds this unknown fear. Wrapping my arms tightly around her body, I gently pressed a kiss on her forehead. Then I looked into her soft eyes with a smile and said "Misha, you taught me what love is. You calm my soul, my heart. The feelings I have for you can't truly be stringed in words, but the only thing I can say is that I have fallen in love with your soul, more than your body and there is no way to turn back from here." Then I gently held her palm and placed it on the left side of my chest and continued "Can you hear the beats Misha? Just remember, they can never lie!"

Tears of happiness rolled down from her eyes as she snuggled herself in my arms and said, "You are the best thing that has happened to me, I love you so much!"

We made love again, until we fell asleep in each other's arms.

That night will always be the most precious night of my life. I love her so much!

Coming back to the present day, our lives are humming the best songs, and we can't really get enough of each other. Now as we stay together, our lives have pretty well intertwined with one another, and it feels like we were meant to be together since eternity. For adding some more adventure to our lives, we have planned a trip to Dharamshala, Himachal Pradesh. We are going tomorrow, Saturday for 5 days and we are pretty excited about it. It's being our first trip together, we have planned a lot, regarding the local food, café options, trekking options, and lots more.

"Rishi, I have asked you for the towel 5 minutes back! Where are you?"

Misha's voice brought me back to the present. "Sorry, I just forgot. Let me give you."

I quickly go to the washroom and knock her door. She opens it and drags me inside. "Misha, I am wearing clothes, let me open them at least" I keep telling, but she pushes me below the shower, and I get completely drenched! "This is your punishment for being late in giving my towel!" Saying this she starts laughing aloud. I always surrender myself before her smile, and today is no exception. We both take shower together, where we made wild love under the shower. *Life is really pretty!*

We pack our bags in the rest of the evening, had Rajma Chawal for dinner. We decided to sleep early today, as we need to start tomorrow at 5 AM. We are going via flight from Hyderabad to Chandigarh, which is at 7.30 AM, and from there we have hired a cab till Dharamshala. Misha belongs from Delhi, me from Chandigarh, so we both love mountains a lot. We both didn't go to Dharamshala till date, so we had chosen this place.

"I am so so excited for tomorrow!" Misha exclaims! "We will plan our next trip with Varun and Shweta, it will be fun too!"

"Yes it will be! Who knows, by then they would be dating each other" I winked.

"Then that would be crazy!" Misha's heart jumped.

We had our dinner and slept early. Our alarm rang at 4 AM. We quickly got ready and booked our cab till the airport. We reached the airport by 5.45 AM. Completing all the formalities and check-in procedure, we reached the boarding gate by 7 AM.

We are flying in next 30 minutes, I whispered to my heart! My happiness has no bounds today.

While boarding the flight, Misha gently squeezed my hands and looked at me with a smile. I know she is happy, and that makes me the happiest.

Hugging her sideways and pulling her slightly towards me I say "Let's go sunshine! Let's make our first trip the best trip of our lives!"

She beamed with happiness.

I beamed witnessing my love's happiness.

Chapter 18

Misha

Amidst the mountains with the love of my life, something which perhaps I never dreamt of too! Pinching myself is not working anymore as I am floating in the clouds of happiness. We reached Chandigarh at 10 AM. Our cab from Chandigarh to Dharmshala is booked for 2 PM this afternoon, and we will reach our hotel by 9 PM. These four hours in between is where we are meeting Rishi's parents as they stay in Chandigarh only, at a distance of 15 minutes from the airport.

I have spoken with Rishi's parents before, and I must admit that they are very cool and nice people. I gel up with them easily, and Aunty is my new partner for diet plans, and she is really cute. She has recently joined a new yoga class and have started sharing her yoga videos with me on a regular basis. I love watching them, and somehow those videos have thrown a positive impact on my brain which now wants to switch to yoga from gym. So, I have planned to join a yoga class post this trip.

As we reach Rishi's place, Aunty and Uncle greets us with open arms. They are warm and lovable, just like my man. His place is a big bungalow with lushes of green and blooming flowers in front of it. The garden has beautiful outdoor chairs and tables, and a pretty swing in one corner. I instantly fell in love with the place. Looking at the garden, my mind runs to a peaceful holiday over here with Rishi where I am reading one of my favorite novels sitting on that swing.

"Do you like this place?" Aunty' s voice dragged me back to the present.

"I love it, Aunty. It's just so pretty! I wonder, how you maintain everything!"

A broad smile appeared on her face as she continued, "When I saw this place for the first time, I instantly fell in love with it. When I said your Uncle, that I want this house to be our home, he agreed in a blink. He just said one thing that, 'Simi we both will make sure to keep this place happy and warm always', and that is how we built this home from scratch."

"It's beautiful Aunty, just like you!" I smiled.

She blinked with happiness.

Next 3 hours we had a hearty scrumptious meal inside the house. I heard some happy childhood memories of Rishi and his younger brother Harsh, who is currently studying in Germany. Uncle's jokes added that icing on the top, and we all had a great time. At 2 PM, our cab arrived, we waved a happy goodbye and started our journey. It will take around 6 hours 45 minutes to reach our hotel in Dharamshala. Rishi cuddled me sideways and asked “So, how excited you are?”

Beaming with joy, I said “Rishi, I can’t even express how happy am I, it’s just as if I feel like a child all over again.”

“You will be happier, once you reach the surprise resort I booked for you.”

Rishi has booked our stay in Dharamshala, and it’s a surprise for me. I tried to know it by various means, but every time I hopelessly failed. Though I have zero regrets for it! I am desperately waiting to reach our destination.

“Rishi, at least now say the name of the resort! We are just few hours away!” I made a puppy face.

“No, never, not possible. It’s a surprise and surprises are not meant to be disclosed!”

I smiled staring at his innocent serious face.

“It seems that tonight is going to be really a special one!” Mini-me made my stomach wobble and I mentally blushed imagining it.

Listening to numerous songs, chatting, and taking small naps, we finally reached our destination at 9.30PM. The resort is in the outskirts of the town, so it took half an hour more to reach there. As our cab parked before the hotel, my eyes bloomed witnessing the beauty in front of me. It’s a tree villa nestled amongst lush green Pine and Deodar trees, surrounded by snowcapped mountains, away from the hustle bustle of the city.

This place felt like a scoop of dream bathing under the moonlight of reality. It's as if, God has engraved a new paradise on Earth, and I am one of those lucky kids who got the opportunity to feel this bliss today.

"Did you like it?" Rishi whispered near my shoulders.

I turned towards him and threw myself in his arms. Hugging him tightly with teary eyes I said "I just love this place Rishi, it's the best place I have ever seen in my life! Thank you so much for bringing me here, you are the best!"

"Anything for that beautiful smile" he kisses my cheek.

I blush under my breath.

As we check in to our room, my eyes leave my body seeing the room. The room is extremely beautiful and cozy. There is wooden flooring throughout, and a big king-sized bed in the middle. A side table is offering a glass vase with pretty flowers in it. There are comfy couches, a big dresser, and all other amenities in the room. But amidst all of this, the most unique part of this room is the huge balcony in front of it. The balcony cradles the heavenly picturesque mountains surrounding it and also has a jacuzzi hot water bath at one side of it. Throwing myself in a hot water bath in between these mountains is something I could have never dreamt of. I kept admiring the room and telling Rishi how beautiful it is. Rishi's happiness could be seen oozing out his eyes, and my love overflows for him.

"How did you find something so serene, Rishi?"

"A lot of research and a lot more love" Rishi winked.

I blushed.

"All my tiredness has suddenly vanished seeing this beauty, and I feel a lot more alive" I declare.

Hugging me tightly from behind and placing a kiss on my bare neck he says, "Let's make these 5 days, the most memorable days of our life."

My heart high-fived with his words.

After having some soupy noodles and wine for dinner, we retire to our bed. Loving each other for a while, eventually we fell asleep. In the lap of mountains, in this beautiful resort, in the arms of the most beautiful man, life seems to be beyond perfect. *Will everything break and fall apart once this dream breaks?* A thread of fear runs through my body. This question hits my mind now and then and I feel the world crashing down in front of my eyes, but then again seeing my man sleeping peacefully beside me pushes that fear deep inside my heart, in one corner.

But the problem is, the fear hides temporarily but never vanishes out of my system.

Next morning starts by witnessing the most beautiful sunrise from our balcony. We have decided to explore locally today by enjoying local food and culture. So, we started our day by exploring some local breakfast options in the heart of Himalayas. We tried traditional Nepalese breakfast, and we loved it! Our breakfast included Chiya (Nepalese Tea), Jeri Swari (Funnel Cake With Flatbread), Gorkhali Toast (Spiced Toast) and

Malpuas (Deep Fried Pancakes). The Nepalese restaurant was extremely heartwarming and beautiful.

For the rest of the day, we visited some monasteries, had a special Himalayan thali for lunch, sat on the fields surrounded my hills, and watched the prettiest sunset together. As the sun was going back to his home, it threw it's perfect smile before hiding behind the hills and life seemed to be perfect at that very moment. I kept my head on Rishi's shoulder as he wrapped his arm around me, and we both found a new home in each other's heart this evening.

We also did some shopping in the mall road where we found some beautiful wooden home décor items. Now as we both are living together, I always try to pour my love in my interior décor to make our home more beautiful and happier. So, we shopped for few wooden décor items, an antique lamp for our bedroom and some gifts for Varun and Shweta. We are constantly sharing our pictures from the trip with them in our common WhatsApp group and they like it a lot. We have a hinge that something is going on between Varun and Shweta, but we are waiting for them to confront us with their feelings. If our intuition turns to be true, then it would be the happiest news for our lives.

After having dinner at a local café, we reached our resort at 9 PM.

Our legs have started to retire from our body, but our souls are beaming with happiness. As, I throw myself on the bed, Rishi exclaims "Today was perfect, isn't it?"

"Can't agree more, it was beautiful" I join.

"Tomorrow would be more exciting! We are going for our much-awaited Triund Trek!" He jumped with excitement.

Rishi loves trekking and this would be my very first trekking experience, so definitely it's quite special for us.

"Yaaaay! I would barely sleep tonight, due to my excitement" I exclaimed.

Next few minutes went on discussing our fits for tomorrow, keeping everything ready beforehand as our cab is booked for morning 8 AM. It will take us to McLeod Ganj town from where we will be starting our trek with a group of trekkers. I chose my favorite white sneakers for tomorrow and kept it aside before going back to bed. My lips are sealed with a goofy smile as I lie on bed reminiscing the beautiful memories since yesterday. Rishi cuddles me from behind and kisses my back. My eyes instantly gets filled with sleep along with my happy heart.

This trip is definitely going to be the best trip of my life! I whispered to myself before going back to the land of dreams.

Chapter 19

Rishi

A mist of happy emotions formed a fog in my eyes, as I found Misha sleeping peacefully beside me in the lap of mountains. I never ever thought that such a beautiful girl inside out would come in my life and paint it with happy colors. Generally, people say "Dreams turned into reality" but whenever my eyes fall on Misha, I choose to say, "My reality turned into dreams!"

Today we both are overly excited, as we are going for our much-awaited Trek- Triund Trek. It would be the first-time trekking experience for Misha, so she is full of enthusiasm. We are supposed to start our trek at 7 AM, so we left the hotel at 5.30 AM. As we sat in our cab, Misha smiled at me with her twinkling eyes and said, "These white shoes are pretty, isn't it?"

She has bought a new pair of sneakers few months back, and since then she is in love with them!

"Today your white shoes are turning into brown" I laughed.

"Then you will be buying me the exact same pair" she added.

"Gladly, I will do that" I pass a happy smile.

We reached the starting point of Triund Trek, which is Galu temple, located in McLeod Ganj. Being the starting of March, the temperature is comparatively tilting towards the colder side, and it's around 10 degrees right now. We have worn jackets and joggers which are keeping us warm. The trek length is around 11 kms from here and we will be returning by evening. We have also opted for camping at our destination point where we could rest and enjoy for an hour.

With a group of trekkers, we started our hike at 7.30 AM. According to the locals, we are supposed to reach the top by next 5 hours if we hike at a decent speed.

Holding Misha's hand, I started the hike. The first five kilometers are relatively easy, as compared to the next five. We were at a good speed as both of us are fond of walking. Within 10 minutes of the hike, we were on the outskirts of town with tree-covered paths. As the enthusiasm is quite high in the first few kilometers of the hike, so Misha insisted on clicking few pictures of landscape and us. Undoubtedly she is very excited as this is her first hike, and I am happy to witness this with her. The trekking route offered beautiful rhododendron and oak trees which made it quite picturesque.

After next few kilometers, we found a café where few trekkers have been already having Maggie and tea. So, we took a halt, had Maggie and tea, and then resumed our hike. This café offered astounding views of Dhauladhars and Kangra valley.

The next section was quite tough though, as we went through the forests, the slopes became steeper.

"Rishi let's stop for few minutes, I can't breathe" Misha's voice trembled.

I held her tightly and made her sit under a tree. "Sit here and have some water. Let's rest for a while before we hike again" I exclaimed.

We both were sweating despite the weather being cold. Sitting under the tree, we rested for around 15 minutes after which Misha said, "Let's go Rishi, we need to be with the group."

"You are feeling better now?" I asked concerned.

"Yes, yes now I am feeling good. Come on, let's go."

We resumed our journey again. Along our hike, we had conversations with other group members who have travelled from various parts of India. Meeting new people from different cultures and backgrounds was really fulfilling. As we went up, the view of Mcleod Ganj from the top along with snowcapped mountains all around was indeed breathtaking. Each section from here became steeper and it required a lot of stamina to complete the climb.

After 5 hours of climbing, we finally reached our campsite at 12.30 PM. It's the top of the Triund hill which offers majestic views and vanishes the tiredness in a blink of an eye. We already had our camp booked there, where we rested for an hour, enjoying with the view, peaceful gushes of winds and some music played in our EarPods. We took lot of pictures and shared them in our social media platforms too!

Life seemed to be straight out of a Bollywood movie!

We also had our lunch in a café on the top, before we decided to return back. The trekking group got divided in two halves, one of which decided to do an overnight camping and then hike for another few kilometers till Lahesh cave and then to Indrahar pass, and the other group which included us decided to come back. As it was the first hiking experience for Misha, so we had decided beforehand that we won't stress ourselves, and thus return back by tonight.

We started our way back from there at around 2 PM. This journey was relatively easier than before, and after pacing ourselves a little more than before, we reached Galu temple at around 6 PM.

Our hearts were filled with overwhelming emotions. "Rishi, thank you so much for making me experience this! We will go for more such trekking, I just loved this day!" Misha jumped like a child.

"We will go for trekking every year from now on! Finally, I have got a partner for hiking, love you Misha" I held her tightly.

Throwing both her hands up on the air she said "Yes we will do this every year! Yaaay!"

We have hired a cab for taking us back to our resort. It will take around 40 minutes to reach our destination, so we relaxed ourselves in the back seat of the cab. The driver played some Himalayan music which soothed our hearts as Misha rested her head on my shoulders. After few minutes Misha announced "Let's have tea at some hillside café"

I agreed in a blink.

The driver parked the cab opposite to a small tea stall. We asked the driver, if he wants to have something, to which he denied. We left our backpacks in the car and crossed the road to reach the café.

After ordering 2 cups of tea, we sat in two chairs, witnessing the cool breeze and calmness of the hills. After 10 minutes, we got up and went to the shop owner to pay for the tea. Checking the wallet, I found only a two hundred rupees note in it, as I asked for change the shop owner declined. Misha also checked her wallet, but it had only a five hundred rupees note.

"Wait, I have some loose cash in the side chain of my backpack, let me bring them." Misha said.

"You stay here, I will bring it" I added.

"Rishi, the cab is just on the other side of the road, you stay here, I will just come back in a minute."

Saying this she started walking. After few steps she turned towards me and passed a sweet smile, and at that very second I could see a car running at a high-speed, moving towards her, I call her name frantically from behind "Misha, there is car coming, Move backkkkk" I run towards her to drag her back, but it's too late by then.

Blood everywhere..

Pool of blood..

My Misha, where is my Misha?

She is lying in a pool of blood in front of my eyes.

My Misha..

"Sir, Sir, can you hear me, we need to take her to the hospital, she is alive" A faded voice hits my brain as I could see few people gathering in front of my girl.

I took support from a stranger to stand up on my feet. With shaking legs and soul, I reach her.

Blood everywhere..

My Misha..

I sit on the road and stare at her face. The most beautiful face on this planet. Her forehead has a cut, through which blood is oozing out. "Her right leg is highly injured, don't know if it can be repaired." I hear someone's voice from the crowd. My eyes shift towards her legs, and all I could see is blood, blood, and blood.

My eyes suddenly fall on a blood wrapped white sneaker, lying at a distance and I can't hold myself any longer. I cry and cry my heart out.

"Call the ambulance".

"We need to take her to the hospital fast".

Distant voices echoes in the air, and all I want to do is rewind my life for few minutes and stop Misha from crossing the road. A hand touches my back when I turn back to see someone standing behind me. He stretches out his hand towards me and says "You need to get up, young man! It's time to be brave, she is still alive. Let's take her to the hospital and hope for the best, come with me!" I look at him with tearful eyes, my mind is still trying to register his words. I could see him holding our backpacks in his hand which was left in the cab.

With trembling hands, I picked up Misha in my arms. She is sleeping like an angel. Her right leg has endured the maximum damage, which is full of blood and flesh coming out from it. My legs tremble and I tend to fall, when that unknown man helped me again and held me tightly. We took Misha to his car and ran as fast as we can to the nearest Dharamshala Hospital.

In the next 15 minutes, they took Misha away from me. I shouted, and cried but they didn't allow me to go inside the emergency room. Helplessly I sat on the floor outside the emergency room waiting for the love of my life. "Have some water, you look terrible" the unknown man stood in front of me with a glass of water. Gathering all my courage, I finally said to him "I don't know your name but thank you for helping me in this situation" He sat beside me and put his hand on mine and said "I have lost my wife 2 years back in a terrible road accident. I know how it feels to lose the most important person of your life, and I don't want you to feel the same."

His words threw out all my pain at once and I hugged him and cried my heart out. He rubbed my back and tried to calm me down. "She will be okay, trust me, she will be fine very soon".

With tears rolling on my words, I said "You know, my Misha is invincible. She will fight it!"

He smiles and adds "She will, your love is there with her." In the next few minutes, I get to know that his name is Shreyash, and he is travelling from Delhi. Ever since his wife has left this world, he can't stay at his empty house for more than few months. He needs to travel around, to keep his mind sane. Shiver runs through my spine as I think about my girl. It's been an hour now, when will the doctors say something?

After half an hour a doctor comes out from the ward, and I run towards him. He looks at me and says, "You are with the patient, right?" I want to say the doctor that, my Misha is not a patient, she can't be one, but only thing I could do is nod my head.

"How is she doctor?" I panic.

"She is unconscious right now, due to huge loss of blood. She being A+, we have easily found a match in the blood bank, and blood transfusion has already started, But there is a problem.."

I look at him with fear-filled eyes and ask, "She will be alive, right?"

"Yes, don't worry she will be alive. But the damage in her right leg is quite critical. We are not that well equipped hospital to provide you the best treatment, so I want her to be shifted to Chandigarh, which would be nearest from here and she will get a good treatment over there. We have already arranged an ambulance so without wasting any more minutes, I guess you should take her to Chandigarh."

My head starts spinning again, and I can't figure out what to say. Shreyash came into rescue, he replies to the doctor on my behalf "We will be starting from here right away. Thank you so much Doctor."

The next one hour went in a jiffy, I don't know exactly what happened, I just remember sitting in the ambulance along with Misha. Shreyash has handled everything, he has also managed to collect our luggage from the resort. I can't be more thankful to him for coming like an angel into our lives right now. Before the ambulance was about to start I turn to see Shreyash standing few feet away from the door.

I get off from the ambulance and walk towards him. Holding his hands, I manage to say, "Thank you for everything man, you were a blessing."

He smiles and adds "I will pray for her speedy recovery, she will be fine very soon. If you need any help, you have my number with you, please don't hesitate to call."

"I won't hesitate. Once Misha is fine, we will come to Delhi to visit your place." I sounded hopeful.

"I will eagerly wait for that day" he added with a smile.

I bid him a goodbye before going back to the ambulance. I sat beside Misha and look at her angelic face. Something happened inside me at that very moment which made me say to myself "Whatever it takes, Misha will recover soon. I will make every effort to bring my girl back with a smile. Yes I will do it."

A flame of hope starts flickering in my heart, as the ambulance starts its journey.

"You are not alone Misha, I am there to fight with you. We will win this war, together." I whisper.

Chapter 20

Rishi

7 hours of wait just to hear her voice again.

7 hours of my heartbeat hitting my head with a thud.

7 hours of nonstop prayers of her loved ones.

7 hours of us, staring at that red light of the operation theatre.

My Misha is in the operation theatre for the last 7 hours, and I am helplessly standing at the doorstep of the OT, waiting for a chance to meet my girl.

We are in Fortis Chandigarh for the last 10 hours. Dr. Malini is the one who is looking after Misha's case. We reached here at around 4 AM, today, and after that I don't know how the seconds and minutes had it's pace in the clock. They took Misha to the operating theatre at around 7 AM. As Dr. Malini was about to enter the theatre I ran to her with my raging beats.

"Hi, Doctor, can you please spare 2 minutes? I am really scared and worried about Misha, can you please tell me how she is?" Tears rolled down my eyes, as I tried to join the words and form this sentence before her.

Staring at me for 2 seconds, she finally replied saying "She had a deep cut in the forehead, which needed stiches but mainly we are concerned about her right leg. It has undergone multiple fractures and there is nerve and tissue damage too. Also, taking into consideration that she had a huge amount of blood loss, we need to have an operation immediately. I am the Head of the Orthopedics department here, and I have few more doctors from other departments joining with me, and we will together conduct this surgery."

I stared at her with blank eyes, trying to articulate my words, as my head is spinning at a tremendous speed at this moment. Gathering my courage, I spoke "Will she be able to walk again, Doctor?"

Putting her hand on my shoulder, she said "She will be able to stand up again, it's my promise."

Saying these golden words, she rushed into the Operation theatre and the Red light threw the most difficult times on my eyes.

It's been 7 hours since then, the clock is ticking 1.45 PM right now. I didn't have a working mind to inform anyone about Misha post reaching here. Before taking Misha to the operation Theatre, the Hospital authorities asked me to fill certain forms, where I had to add details of her parents. That's when I realized that I have forgot to inform anyone about her. So, at around 7.30 AM, I informed Misha's, and my parents about her. They are in shock, but I have tried to calm them down. My parents have reached here by 8 AM, and Misha's parents, Mira Aunty and Shaurya Uncle will reach by 2 PM. We all are silently praying with hope and tears in our eyes, just wanting the charm of our life to smile all over again.

After the most difficult 7 hours of our life, the red light went off, and our heart beats stopped alongwith. I could see with my hazy eyes that the door opens, and Dr. Malini comes out, I run towards her with fear and hope in my eyes.

"Doctor, How is my Misha? Tell me she is fine, right?"

She stops and turns back towards me with a serious expression hanging on her face. Taking a deep breath, she says "Look Rishi, the operation was not an easy one. We performed an Open Reduction and Internal Fixation also called ORIF procedure for the Femur or thigh bone which was broken in 2 pieces. We have fixed it with the help of titanium plates and screws. Also, she had tendon and ligament tear in the ankle along with some nerve damage, which had to be operated and fixed. So, overall, it was a complicated procedure, which is successfully done from our end, but.."

She pauses and looks and me.

I try to swallow my tears and say "Please continue Doctor, I am prepared to hear everything".

She says "Look Rishi, even though the operation is successful, it will take several months for her to heal completely, both mentally and physically. She needs to believe in herself to stand up on her feet once again. We will put her into post operative rehabilitation after few days and it will continue for 2-3 months. But after that, she needs to be brave and strong to battle with the circumstances."

I stare at her with blank eyes.

She continues "And one more thing Rishi, the recovery period might be quite long, depending on her body responding to the medicines. So, it might take up to a year for her to walk properly."

My throat feels jammed, refusing words to bubble up. I just look at her without my lips weaving any word.

"Rishi, are you listening to me, Rishi?" Dr. Malini pats my shoulder and tries to bring me back to my senses.

Gathering up all my strengths I manage to say "Doctor, Misha will walk, run, and dance within few months, she will do it! I will make her do it!"

Doctor smiles and says "That's the spirit my boy! Just be by her side always."

"Thank you Doctor for giving me my Misha back, I will forever be indebted to you." I say with tears streaming down my cheeks.

"She is very lucky to have survived after such a horrific accident. She is indeed God's child" Dr. Malini smiles. "You can meet her after 1 hour, once she is shifted to her ward" she adds.

I will be able to see her, touch her, hug her! My heart jumped and kissed my soul.

Everything is going to be alright Misha, I am coming to you, I cry.

"Rishi, where is Misha, how is she now?" Tensed voices coated with tears startle me from behind. I turn back and face the torn faces of Misha's parents.

"Aunty, Uncle, Misha is out of danger now! The operation went successfully, and she will be transferred to the ward in next 1 hour." I try to infuse hopes in their hearts. I explained them everything in next half an hour, subtracting the facts that Dr. Malini said to me post operation. My mother is trying to console Aunty and my dad and Uncle is also trying to hide their fears deep inside their hearts. I am hopelessly checking my watch and waiting for the nurses to bring Misha out of the OT and take her to the ward.

It's 3.30 PM now, Misha has just been shifted to her ward, and we all have gathered around her. The girl who was jumping with joy and trekking with fun 20 hours ago, is now lying in a bed covered with bandages and filled with sorrow. I couldn't stare at her for more than a minute, my heart ripped apart from my body and tears started rolling down my eyes. For the first time in my life, I am feeling so helpless, unable to do anything for the person I love the most. It's an unusual and unfathomable pain, that's running in my veins hopelessly.

Misha has opened her eyes, and she is trying to understand the situation around her. Due to anesthesia and heavy doses of sedatives, she is not in her fully conscious state. Her parents and my parents are trying to talk with her, but she is just staring blankly and nodding her head sometimes. I couldn't look at her like this, I am having this constant feeling of fighting with time and running back to yesterday, where I can just hug her tightly and refrain her from crossing the road. My guilt is eating me up, and I have given myself the award of the worst person in this world.

I waited for everyone to meet her, so I could be alone with her for few minutes. As everyone left the ward, I sit in a chair facing her face beside her bed. She is lying, with her eyes closed. Her forehead is covered with a bandage, hiding the stiches and her cute temple. Her right leg is completely covered with cast and bandages, with only her cute toes peeping out from it. I swallow the tear ball in my throat and gently touch her palm. Her palm is cold and soft, just as they used to be always. She opens her eyes feeling my touch and looks at me with those blue eyes filled with emotions, pouring out thousands of words coated with feelings.

"How are you feeling Misha?" I manage to ask with a faded smile.

"Our first trip turned out to be our last one, right?" she asks with blue eyes soaked in water.

"Stop saying such things, you are going to be fit in few months, and we are going to explore the world together. I want to see the world through your eyes, Misha." My teary eyes spoke more than my words.

She stared at me silently, and then closed her eyes saying "I am feeling tired Rishi, I want to sleep"

I could see that tiny drop of water in the brink of her right eye, desperately trying to hold on to her eyelid. My girl is shattered into pieces from within and here I am trying to juggle with words and help her conquer her fears and sorrow. She needs much more from me, she needs me to help her trust herself, she needs me to be the anchor to her heart by protecting it from drifting into the sea of sorrows.

I silently sit there holding her palm in mine and softly kissing it.

"I will bring my Misha back on her feet" I promise to myself.

Chapter 21

Rishi

1 week later

"Rishi, should we try Maggie instead of a sandwich, Misha will definitely love it." Mira Aunty exclaimed.

"Aunty, that's a brilliant idea, we must give it a try" I smile.

"I am making it right away, then" Aunty goes to the kitchen with a smile.

So, Misha and I are at Misha's house in Delhi for the past 6 days. We shifted her from Chandigarh to Delhi after she stayed for 2 days in the hospital. Dr. Malini was very kind and supportive throughout, and she also spoke with the orthopedic department in Fortis Delhi and have arranged Misha's post-surgery rehabilitation which have already started since last 2 days.

Misha had a word with Radhika, her manager and she is really worried about her. When I first met both of them, in my office, I knew that Radhika cared about Misha, she was not like my manager, Naveen, of course! Radhika has asked Misha to take a month's leave and after that if her body permits then she can work from home for any length of time required. I also had a word with Naveen and have applied for 2 months work from home for as of now. As I am handling some major projects which need to be delivered in next 2 months, so he had no choice but to comply with my decision, *even though he didn't want to!* Rohan is also helping me a lot by sharing my workload so I can give more time to Misha. Varun and Shweta are coming here tomorrow and will stay with us for a couple of days. My parents were also here for the first two days, after which they have left for Chandigarh. They will be visiting us again in next few weeks. Everyone adores my girl and is worried about her.

A unanimous prayer from everyone is reaching out to the Almighty every day, I know he will listen to us very soon.

"Can you try to feed her, she is not listening to me" Auntie's voice echoed from Misha's Room.

I hurried towards them and took the bowl from Aunty. "You go and have some rest, I will feed her" I assured her.

Misha is lying, hiding her body and feelings inside the blanket, with only her pale face facing the world out of it. I have seen huge changes in her in the last few days, she is trying to hide herself in a shell and is refusing to face herself anymore. She no longer talks or laughs like before, most of the time she is trying to sleep, *or to run away to a different world maybe.*

I am trying to be with her every second, talk with her, read her books, play music, but everything seems to be hitting against a wall and coming back to me. She remains silent, with her void gaze. Seeing her like this silently eats up my heart from within. I have not slept for days, as I keep on rewinding that minute when Misha was about to cross the road and that car….

That car, that blue colored car came flashing in front of my eyes for hundreds of times. It had escaped within a blink after the accident, and I was not in a state to remember the vehicle number. I tried replaying that scene in my mind, just in case I visualize the number, but every time I see Misha's face in those scenes, I reach a dead end.

Sitting in the edge of the bed beside her face, I put my palm on her forehead.

"Misha, you need to eat something, let me feed you".

"I am not a baby Rishi, I can eat myself" Misha's stern voice pierced through my ears.

"Yes, of course you can have it yourself. I will just help you to sit back.." I started holding her back and making her sit.

She held my hand and moved it away angrily. "Can every one of you stop making me feel like a handicapped? I can very well sit up on my own" The anger in her eyes was filled with pain and despair as she sits up on the bed.

"Stop saying whatever you want Misha, neither you are a handicapped nor anyone wants to make you feel that way, and you already know that very well!" my eyes are filled with pain. Misha gives a sideways look and continue scrolling her phone without uttering a single word.

"Baby, I just want you to have this bowl of Maggie, you need to eat something. You have not eaten anything since afternoon."

"I know what to do, you don't have to teach me." She twists her lips without looking at me.

"Can you stop being so rude?" I glare.

"Can you stop staying at my house and try to look after me?" Misha spits volcano through her words and I am left dumbstruck.

"Misha, are you in your senses or not, do you know what you are saying?" Auntie's voice startle both of us as she stands at the door with a glass of juice in her hand.

"Mom, you were eavesdropping?" Misha asks with a stern voice.

"No, I was not. I just came to give you this juice and I heard you saying such insensible and rude things to Rishi".

"Aunty, it's completely fine. Misha is not in a good mood today, that's why she said such things which she didn't mean actually, I know it very well." I can read empathy in Misha's eyes as I speak with Aunty.

"But still, Misha should not say such things to you. You are the one who is tirelessly taking care of her since last 8 days. You are a blessing for her, Rishi" I can see tear in corner of Auntie's eyes.

"I am not a kid, I can very well take care of myself" Misha replies angrily without looking at both of us.

"Don't know what has happened to this girl, she was never like this before" Aunty gasps a breath and keeps the glass on the table and turns back to leave the room.

"Don't worry Aunty, I will talk with her. You go and have some rest" I try to comfort her. She throws a weak smile towards me before leaving the room.

I am also in a similar situation like Aunty regarding Misha's case. She is behaving in a completely different manner since last few days, and I can't recognize her anymore. She is no more that sweet, caring girl. Somewhere or the other, I am having a weird feeling that she is trying to avoid my presence in her life, I am the one who is creating problems for her, and she is clearly annoyed with me. But why? Does she blame me for the accident? Does she think that I could have saved her?

She is not wrong, right? Is that so, that I could have saved her? My head starts hurting and eyes starts burning.

"Rishi, are you okay?" Misha touches my shoulder.

I turn towards her and look into her eyes. Her eyes are soft and filled with tears, wanting to say something. "Don't you love me anymore, Misha?" my heart throws the most difficult question.

"A lot of things have changed Rishi, I don't know what I want or feel anymore" She replies softly.

I couldn't hold myself any longer. I hug her tightly with all my strength, as if my soul wants to get attached with hers. "Don't say all these Misha, everything will be alright very soon. Just don't lose your trust from this relationship, it means everything to me." I keep crying and she remains silent. I continue with my tears "If you feel that I am the one responsible for everything, then punish me as you want Misha, I deserve it. Just don't distance yourself from me, I will not be able to live without you" I cry my heart out, but she doesn't say a single word. I can hear her sobbing, I can feel her pain, but I am unable to do anything about it.

I sit back straight, hold her shoulders tightly and look into her eyes. Why is it that every time I found these eyes easily readable and it's just now that I am unable to decipher a single word out of them. What are they trying to say?

"Misha, is there something which is bothering you?"

"There is nothing Rishi, you are just overthinking" she replies without looking at me.

"There is something, I know that very well, please tell me Misha, please" I beg.

"Can you please pass my medicine box?"

"Yes sure" I take the blue colored medicine box from the bed side table and hand it over to her.

"Misha, are you worried about your leg? I spoke with Dr. Aarti, the Head of Orthopedic department in Fortis Delhi, who is handling your case now and she said you will be completely fine within next 6 months" I sound hopeful.

She silently takes out a medicine from a strip and gulps it down with the orange juice that Aunty left few minutes back.

"Also, from tomorrow your new physiotherapy sessions starts which will continue for 2 months. It will help you a lot Misha. I will be there with you at every step of it" I continue to speak and feel as if I am talking to myself. She is silent and expressionless.

Keeping the box aside, she lies down on the bed and closes her eyes saying "I am feeling sleepy Rishi, please let me sleep. We can talk tomorrow."

"I just.." before I could complete my sentence, she adds "Please turn off the lights before leaving the room."

Why is she behaving like this? Why is she distancing herself from me?

I slowly get up from the bed, unfold her blanket and cover her body. Her lips tremble a bit, but her eyes remain closed. I caress her hair with my fingers and place a gentle kiss on her forehead. "Goodnight Misha, I love you." I say before I leave her room.

I don't know this girl, she can't be my Misha. Something is definitely bothering her a lot, and I have to find it out as soon as possible. If she wants to punish me, I am gladly ready for enduring everything, but I just want her to be the girl she used to be. That happy, loving soul.

I want my love, I want my Misha back.

But the question is, does she want me to be with her anymore? Does she still love me?

Chapter 22

Misha

Void, yes that's the word.

The world seems to be a void place in front of my eyes.

"Her leg will never be like before, she won't be able to jump or run easily after this!"

I overheard the Doctors having this conversation in the operating room. Yes, they tried injecting me with strong sleeping pills, after giving an anesthesia for the lower part of my body. But those sleeping pills felt weaker before my fear. I was awake somehow in the middle of the operation, and I heard the doctors saying that my leg won't be like the one it used to be.

No, I didn't say this to anyone, except uttering this line in my mind for thousands of times like a prayer.

That second of my life when that blue colored car came running towards me.

The blue colored car, blood, Rishi, pain, blue sea, suffocation..

I start sweating again. Panic runs through my body, and I start crying.

I check the phone, it's 4 AM.

This happens every day, every night. I have this feeling that I am drowning in a sea, I am shouting and asking for help, I am trying to breathe, but I can't.

I am feeling suffocated, I am feeling dying.

"Rishi, where are you? Rishi, Rishi" I keep shouting helplessly.

"I am here Misha, I am coming, I will not let you die" Rishi jumps into the sea and tries to save me. But he can't. Because, he doesn't know how to swim, and so do I.

So, ultimately we both die, drowning in this massive blue sea.

But I love my Rishi too much and I can't let him die. This feeling of seeing Rishi dying in front of me, because of me, is eating me up. How can I do this to him?

I want him to run away from me. I don't want him to suffer my fate, he didn't do anything wrong, right? Since the time I have heard those doctors saying that I won't be walking and running like before, I have decided that I need to protect Rishi from my fate. He needs to run away. He doesn't deserve to be sacrificing his life taking care of someone like me, he deserves much more than that, he deserves the world. He is too good for me, he can't waste his life, his happiness for the sake of my destiny. I want him to find someone with whom he can dance through his life, someone with whom he can jump up in joy, someone to travel the world with, someone who can walk by his side throughout his life.

I am not that someone.

I will destroy his happiness, his life, with my disabilities, with my weak leg.

So, I am trying hard to push him away from me. This is something which is choking my soul from within, but I have no other choice. Whenever I see him, I see his love for me in his eyes, I see myself failing more and more in front of him. I want him to dislike me, to hate me, to leave me, but he is not doing that.

If you ask me how I feel, when I behave rudely with him, or how I feel when I don't answer his innocent questions and try to ignore him, it's the same feeling as you are stabbing yourself with a knife repeatedly and crying out in pain. He means the world to me, and to see my world sinking in sorrow, is like punishing myself to death.

I ask the almighty the same question every day, "Why did you choose me, what was my mistake?

Silence. That's what resonates in the air, in return to my question.

I check the clock, it's 6 AM.

Another 24 hours without sleep.

Another 24 hours of planning ways by which Rishi will start hating me.

Another 24 hours of thinking why God chose to keep me alive after the accident.

Another 24 hours of hating myself even more.

"Misha look who have come to meet you!" Rishi's voice jingled from the door.

"Hey Misha, how are you?" familiar voices echoes, as I could see Shweta and Varun standing in front of me.

Don't know why, my tears dwell down my eyes and I start crying profusely by seeing them. Maybe something which I was trying to hold back in the past few hours.

Shweta runs towards me, sits beside me, and hugs me tightly. "Misha, we all are here now, you will be fine very soon, don't cry please, I love you".

I know she is crying too, I know she knows that I won't be fine very soon, but still, everyone who loves me gives me these false hopes, to cheer me up. I try to comply with their feelings and put on a fake smile to make them happy.

"It's okay, I am completely fine. Just that seeing you two idiots after so long, made me emotional" I smile looking at them.

"You can call Varun an idiot, but I am not. You know right? that I am a star" Shweta laughs.

"Yes, you wish" Varun laughs.

From the corner of my eyes, I could see Rishi standing and looking at me. I know what he is thinking right now, that how come I am behaving nicely with them and not with him, I know he is blaming himself for my behavior, but I have to do it anyway as I have no other choice.

When Rishi was asking me yesterday, that do I blame him or not for everything, is that the reason for my odd behaviors, I wanted to hug him tightly and shut his lips with a kiss, saying that he is always a blessing for me. Because of him, I have got this second life, because of him I have learnt the meaning of love. But I can't say anything because I don't want him to love me anymore.

Putting an arm around Varun's shoulder Rishi says, "Thank you guys for coming, at least there is a glimpse of smile on Misha's face, which we have not seen in last 9 days!"

"Now that we are here for 5 days, we will cheer up our girl and lighten up her mood, right Misha?" Shweta looks at me with cheerful eyes. She continues looking at my eyes for few seconds, as if she is trying to gather some information from them.

Mom enters the room with cold drink and snacks and puts them in the corner table. "Shweta and Varun, please have something and make yourself comfortable." Mom smiles.

"Aunty, you don't have to do all these, we are not here to overload you with more responsibilities, we want to help and do our best Aunty" Shweta holds mom's hand.

"Yes Aunty, consider us as family and allow us to help you all in this situation" Varun joins.

"Okay, okay I am not doing anything, consider this as your own home and just let me know if you need something." Mom says with smiles and tears in her eyes.

I hate that all of them is struggling just for me, I hate myself.

Rishi is silent. Rishi keeps staring at me.

I can feel his stare crawling up my body and seeping in my veins, I want to store this stare forever in my cells, as I don't know if I will be able to swim through my days without him looking at me.

God, I don't even know if I will be able to breathe without him.

It's 10 PM, the day crawled at a faster speed than usual, as Shweta and Varun lightened our air with the hopes in their eyes and smiles on their lips. They all are thinking that I have already slept, so they are talking at a minimal volume. Nobody will ever know that sleep brings back all the bad memories, and I hate closing my eyes, I hate dreaming, I hate everything.

"Misha, I know you are awake, I want to talk with you." Shweta's deep voice shakes me.

I turn towards the other side and see her standing at the side of my bed.

"God, you scared me! I had almost slept!" I try to fake a smile.

"Stop fooling me Misha, I know you better than the rest of the world. Neither you were sleeping, nor you are going to sleep. You are hiding something deep inside your eyes, and I need to know that right now".

She caught me off guard, and I have no chance to escape this situation at this moment. Tears start rolling down my cheeks and I feel like running away, *only if I could.*

Shweta holds me tightly by wrapping her arms around my neck and says "Misha, I am here. Stop crying please, we all are here with you, you are not alone in this."

I look at her with my pale teary eyes and say, "I am the worst person in this world."

"What's wrong with you, why are you saying this?" Shweta has fears in her eyes.

I take support of her hand and slightly turn towards her saying "You know, I have ruined that person's life who has actually taught me to live, love and dream. This guilt is killing me from inside."

"So, you think you are the one for destroying Rishi's life?" Shweta narrows her eyes.

I close my eyes and whisper "Yes obviously, I think so."

"And that is the reason for your cold behavior towards Rishi, right? You just want him to walk away from your life?" Shweta looks at me with her cold eyes.

"Yes, yes, I want him to run away from my awful life. I know, I can't give him all the happiness, I will only burden him up with this leg!" I cry.

"Misha you are such a big fool. Neither you have understood Rishi's emotions, nor you are respecting your love, your relationship. How can you imagine all this when Rishi is the one who is desperately trying to just bring a tint of smile on your face? You think your leg will be the one which will burden his life? Your absence is something which will kill his life and snatch away all the happiness from it, you fool. You are doing such a big mistake Misha, just talk with him and mend everything" Shweta takes a deep breath and wipes off the drop of tear falling on her nose.

"I have heard the Doctors saying that my leg won't be like it used to be, in the long run. I know Rishi loves to travel, he wants to see the world, and I will be the one obstructing that vision for him. I will not be able to do that Shweta, I love him way too much!"

Shweta looks at me with her mind somewhere else. She remains silent.

"What happened, why are you not saying anything?" I ask.

"Nothing, I think I am overstepping in your life. It's after all your life and your decision, so you would better know how you want things to turn into! But whatever it is, my love for you will always remain the same sweetie." She gives me a hug.

How come she changed her mind all of a sudden? Is she hiding something from me?

"You are overthinking Misha, as always!" mini-me reminded me with a slap.

I swiped away the thread of thought and took a deep breath. I am glad that she understood my situation. As I know, if she tried to convince me more for changing my mind, then I would have given up and bring my love back into my life. *Because that is something, which I am dying to do since last few days!*

"Remember, you are not saying anyone a word about this, especially Rishi" I exclaim.

"Yes, I know, I won't do that," She says with a faint smile.

I always thank the Universe for sending me a friend like her in my life.

"I love you, you know that right?" I ask her holding her eyes with mine.

"I love you more" She smiles.

Chapter 23

Rishi

4 days later

I stare at the ceiling as I notice a lizard crawling on the ceiling of the room. I keep staring, with multiple thoughts crawling in my mind, occupying my sleep for tonight.

To be precise, not only for tonight, but for the last couple of days. I came to know about something few days back, which created chains of thoughts inter-mingled among each other, and now I am desperately trying to loosen their knots and walk through my mind. My brain replays that conversation over and over again, which happened with Shweta few days ago.

It was around 11 PM, I was lying on the bed, staring at the wall, and thinking about Misha. It was the same day when Shweta and Varun came here. I was as usual sad, and thinking about why Misha is behaving so rudely with me, while she is being so sweet with Shweta and

Varun. Suddenly I hear a knock at my door. “Who could be at this hour? Is Misha not well?” I have a sudden fear. With a raging heartbeat, I open the door and find Shweta standing in front of me with her eyes filled with tears.

“What happened Shweta, is everything alright with Misha?” Fear rolls through my body.

“Can I come inside? I have to tell you something” She looks at me.

“Please come” I say as she comes inside, and I follow her inside the room.

What would Shweta want to tell me at this odd hour? Why Varun is not with her? My mind runs at a good speed in search of probable answers, but I can’t find any.

“Now you are scaring the shit out of me Shweta, please tell something” I look at her as she sits on the side of the bed.

“Misha is running from you Rishi, don’t let her go” she says.

My heart constricts.

“I think I know, why she wants to run away from me” I say staring at the floor.

“You know?” she frowns.

“She blames me for the accident, and she doesn’t want me to be in her life anymore” I reply holding back my tears.

"You know nothing Rishi, you know nothing!" she cries. "She loves you way too much than you think she does" she continues.

I freeze, listening the last line. What does that even mean? If she loves me then why is she behaving like this?

"Did Misha tell you something?" I finally ask.

Shweta pauses for few seconds and finally say "She thinks, she will eventually burden you up with her injured leg. She feels that she will act as an obstacle in the path of your life, your happiness. Rishi, she has overheard the doctor's saying that her leg can take a longer time to heal, and it may not be as strong as it used to be before. Since then, she is trying to run away from your life for the sake of your happiness, you fool! She confronted me with her feelings today, only because I promised her that I won't utter a single word about this to anyone. But I can't look at my best friend suffering like this, silently, being misunderstood by everyone, especially you. I have seen her going through a heartbreak once, I can't see her going through the same once more. She has already endured enough pain in her life till now!" She takes a deep breath after this.

The world starts spinning, as realization hits my soul and guilt hammers my heart. How can I be such a big fool? I couldn't read her eyes when she needed me the most. "*Shame on you Rishi, shame on your love*" My heart teases me. Tears roll down my cheeks as I replay Shweta's words in my head.

"I have failed her, Shweta. I have failed her miserably." I say as tears bubble up in my throat.

She puts a hand on my shoulder and says "You have time to mend things. But this time, you need to heal Misha's heart, because she is broken from inside."

"I don't know how to confront her, I feel horrible" I say looking at her with teary eyes.

"Take your time mate and find something special for her. She loves you too much Rishi, I have never seen so much love in her eyes for anyone till date." She smiles.

Guilt rips my heart from inside, as if a chisel is cutting some wood.

"I will not let her go, Shweta. I will make her believe in the power of our love. She needs to know, that without her, I am just hollow from inside. She needs to know, that her presence in my life can never burden it up, it will only add wings to my heart, and it will always fly high. She is my energy, she is my everything. She also needs to know that her leg will be fine very soon, she will fight with it putting on her brave smile and stand up again in next few months. I won't let her bear so much pain, she has to be the one, she used to be before." I say with tears coated lines.

"I know Rishi, you will do that. I know how much you love her, I trust you mate." She holds my hands and smiles warmly.

"Thank you for letting me know, Shweta. You are a true friend." I try to smile.

"Just don't rush into speaking with her regarding all of this, she might panic, her mind is not in a good state as of now. Do something special to melt her heart, to bring your girl back to your arms" she adds.

How can I say her, that I just want to run to Misha right now, hug her tightly and wipe away all her fears, all her sadness.

But Shweta is right, I shouldn't rush this time.

"Rishi, I must take your leave now. I need to go upstairs to my room without making a sound as it is already too late, and everyone is asleep" Shweta says.

Shweta and Varun are staying on the first floor of this house, and rest of us on the ground floor.

"Yes, you must go and catch some good sleep. After travelling from Hyderabad today, you must be really tired." I speak. "Also, I can never say you thank you enough for what you did today, you healed our lives, Shweta." I look at her with tears blurring my vision.

"You both owe me a huge treat once you are back to Hyderabad" she winks.

"Deal" I smile.

"Good Night Rishi" she says as she gets up to leave the room.

"Good Night Shweta" I say as she leaves the room.

Thousands of thoughts hit my mind after that. My Misha is in pain, I need to hug her, say her that everything is good, she needs to trust us. But right now, I need to find the right time to confront her, I need to make her feel that I am her safe place, I am her home.

"Misha, I am coming for you" my injured heart sings.

It's been 4 days since this conversation with Shweta. For these 4 days, I have tried acting normal before her, before everyone. Misha's physiotherapy sessions are going on every day, but she seems to be disinterested about everything. Now, I know the reason. She lies on the bed, scrolling her phone mindlessly and sometimes she speaks with Shweta and Varun, but not with me. I don't force her anymore, and I can see the pain in her eyes when she looks at me. It throws a thousand of questions which I will answer very soon. Shweta and Varun leaves day after tomorrow, and everyone in the house is busy about tomorrow. Why? Because it's my girl's birthday!

The day I am waiting for since last few days, the day I want to wipe away all her fears and hug her tightly. So right now, my mind is occupied with the thoughts of how I can make her feel special, how I can heal that beautiful heart, how can I let her know that she is the one who brings sunshine to my life, she is my life. "Well, tomorrow is the day, tomorrow would be the best day of our lives." I smile to myself as I watch the lizard crawl on the ceiling of the room.

Chapter 24

Misha

18th March

The clock ticks 6 AM.

My eyes remain closed, my cheeks remain wet.

Today is my birthday, I turn 29 years old. This birthday was supposed to be my first birthday with Rishi, this birthday was supposed to be one of the most special ones till date.

But, I guess fate has written a different story for me. Happiness repels from my life, and sadness hugs my life tightly, always. I am lying down on my bed, with a leg which I can barely move and with a heart which I can barely understand. Life is playing harsh games with me, and I am just a spectator, watching my sad life from a distance.

When the clock ticked 12 AM today, Mom, Dad, Shweta, and Varun came to my room with a cake and some balloons in their hands. I tried to look happy, but my eyes were searching for that person whom I expected the most, my Rishi. He was not there. I guess, my plan worked, right? He has already started hating me, he is happy without me.

Then, I should be happy, right? But sadly, I am not. Every cell of my body is calling him, every inch of my skin wants to feel his touch, but he is gone. While everyone was singing "Happy Birthday" for me, all I wanted to do is just run away from here, run away to a place where I could just cry, and no one can hear me. *But I can't even walk now.*

The clock ticks 7 AM.

Since the last 7 hours, my eyes are searching for Rishi. But he didn't wish me till now. I don't know whether he is in the house or not. I have last seen him yesterday evening. Since the last 4 days, I have seen some changes in him. He is no longer making efforts to talk with me, or sit beside me, or read for me. I guess he has already moved on, he no longer loves me anymore.

I expected Shweta to scold me, to tell me to go back to Rishi, but she didn't do any of that. She accepted everything very easily. *Sounds strange!*

"This is what you wanted Misha, so better be happy now", Mini-me always tells the truth, no matter how much hurtful it is.

The day is moving slower than usual.

It's 1 PM now. Mom and Shweta have cooked my favorite lunch today. I went to the living room today, sitting on my wheelchair. Shweta said that I should move around the house in my wheelchair more often than usual. It will make me happy. Sadly, it won't. Nothing is making me happy right now. *Why did Rishi give up on me so easily? Why didn't he fight for me?*

It's 3 PM now.

There is no sign of Rishi, anywhere.

My Physiotherapist arrives at 3.15 PM. She asks me, how am I feeling today. I fake a smile and say, I am good.

She wishes me Happy Birthday, I just smile.

She tries new exercises for my leg, but I don't co-operate with her.

It's 6 PM now.

I am lying on my bed, watching a thriller movie on the television, desperately trying to kill time and change today's date. Shweta comes to my room and sits beside me and says "Misha, Uncle and Aunty have decorated the living room for you and have brought a beautiful cake for you. I will help you in getting ready and then we will go and have lots of fun today!"

"I don't want to do all this Shweta, I am really very tired."

"Baby, Aunty and Uncle are waiting for you. Don't ruin their plans now!", Shweta insists.

Half-heartedly, I sit up on my bed holding Shweta's hand. A shriek pain runs through my right leg, as Shweta helps me to change my clothes. I bite my bottom lip to hide the pain. With Shweta's help, I wore a blue colored knee length dress. She insisted me to tame my hair and put on some makeup. I denied at first, but eventually gave in. It's perhaps a week now that I have not properly looked at myself in the mirror. As I looked at my reflection today, I got scared of myself. I look so pale, so weak. Shweta managed to comb my hair and tie it in a ponytail. I put on some light makeup and a pink lip shade. Shweta looks at me with teary eyes and says, "Now you are looking like my beautiful Misha, love you so much, girl."

I look at her and pass a pale smile.

She helps me sit on the wheelchair and starts moving it towards the living room.

Wait, No.., she is not taking me to the living room; she is turning the wheel towards Rishi's room!

My heart started hammering.

Is Rishi here?

I turn back and ask Shweta "Why are you not taking me towards the living room."

She remains silent, hiding a grin.

His room is completely dark and silent.

What the hell is happening here?

Shweta settles my wheelchair at a corner, and turns towards me saying "All the best, honey! We love you."

Saying this, she leaves the room, and closes the door from behind. I sit there, clueless.

Suddenly there is light inside the room. Wait, No, it's more than just light! The entire ceiling and walls of the room get filled with stars, and planets, as if I am sitting at the center of THE UNIVERSE!

The stars are moving in the ceiling and throwing beautiful lights on the floor. Words can't even describe what my eyes were witnessing at that very happy second. Suddenly these lines of Prateek Kuhad starts playing in the background.

Maybe it's the way that you breathe in me
Maybe it's the man that you see in me
Maybe it's the fragrance of your hair
Yeah, I just wanna kiss you when you're there.

I just want you all around me, baby
Can we make that happen, please?

Goosebumps run through my body. It is Rishi, he is somewhere around me, "Rishiiii" I call out his name frantically.

The door crackles. I look towards the door, only to find my Man, My Rishi standing there with a smile on his face.

He comes near me and kneels down before the wheelchair. Holding my palm in his, he starts saying, "You know, Misha, you always kept telling me that how lucky you are that I came into your life and helped you to conquer your fears, your demons. But have you ever asked me what I found in my life after you came into it?"

I swallow my tears and look at him, as he continues "Misha, you brought emotions to my life which I never knew existed, you made me mature, caring, passionate and You created this MAN, who is sitting down before you. Without you, I am nothing Misha. You think that you will become a burden for me with your leg? How can you be such a big fool Misha? I have seen an entire Universe in those blue eyes, the first time I saw them. With you, every part of this world is heaven for me, with you I can do everything."

"It's just that Rishi, I don't want you to compromise on anything.." before I could complete, Rishi puts a finger on my lips and says "When I am with you, I am the Happiest. I am never compromising on anything, and without you I am compromising on everything. Misha, can I ask you something? Will you honestly answer me?"

I nod my head with blinking tears.

"Why do you always feel that you are alone in your struggles? Why can't you trust me and shed all your fears on me?"

"I don't know, I am just scared that you will leave me if I do that" I say biting my lips.

"That's because, you don't fully understand my feelings for you. Misha, I want to be with you in your hard times as much as I want to root for you in your good times. Have faith in our love baby, we together can heal and conquer, every obstacle in life. You will stand up on your feet very soon, that's my promise. Just trust 'US' and tell yourself that we can win this together. We will make the Impossible, Possible, my love. Love can create magic Misha, you just need to jump into it".

A big rock vanishes through my chest, and suddenly I feel so happy, so light, so contended. Why didn't I think about all these before?

I put my palm on his and say, "I love you so much Rishi, and I am sorry for everything."

Caressing my palm with his fingers, he says "You don't have to be sorry, you just need to trust me baby. Look above you, these stars, these planets symbolizes our Universe, our own little Universe. You are my Home Misha, you are my everything."

Tears roll down my eyes, as I throw myself on his chest. He covers me with his long hands and presses his chin on my head. After few seconds, he loosens himself from me and then holds my face with his palms. Looking at me with his love filled eyes, he says "Misha, I have something for you, I have thought about it a lot, and I know that this time is the best time for it."

What is he referring to? A jolt of questions run through my heart.

He puts his hand in the back pocket of his Jeans and takes out a small red box wrapped with ribbon.

My chest is pounding, my heart is jumping.

Opening the box, he takes out the most beautiful diamond ring, I have ever seen in my life. Taking my hand in his, he says "Are you ready to spent your life in a roller coaster ride with me? I know, I might have flaws but my love for you is unadulterated, it is pure."

I look at him with my face filled with emotions as I say with a big smile pasted on my face "I was never so sure about anything before, I am waiting to spend my life with an idiot like you."

He puts the ring on my finger, and it beautifully cuddles my finger, my hand, my heart. As, if they already knew about this since a long time.

"This ring is so beautiful, I love you so much Rishi."

He brings my face closer to his and whispers "I love you more than anything baby, I love you a lot", then he locks his lips with mine and I fly into the world of dreams.

I have never been happier than this moment! I have finally reached my home.